Watching the Detectives is Julian Rathbone's eleventh
thriller. It forms part of a trilogy featuring Brabt and
Commissioner Jan Argand. The other titles in the trilogy
are *Base Case* and *The Euro-Killers*.

Pluto Crime

Edited by Ronald Segal

'. . . Is there anything inherently illogical with the concept of socialist – or, at least, politically and socially aware – crime fiction? Pluto Press, publishers of serious left wing books, have inaugurated a crime list to prove that the two can mix . . . the first batch of pinko whodunits augers well for the genre.' *The Times*

'. . . Sturdily resisting the temptation to call the series Red Herrings, the editors begin promisingly with four quite different types of thriller, varied in their setting and in the way politics enters into the action, but all taking an intelligent readership for granted . . .' *The Bookseller*

'. . . the most innovative publishing experiment of the crime-story year!' *The Guardian*

Julian Rathbone

Watching
the Detectives

Pluto Press

London and Sydney

First published in 1983 in Great Britain by Michael Joseph Ltd,
44 Bedford Square, London WC1

This edition published in Britain in 1985 by Pluto Press Limited,
105a Torriano Avenue, London NW5 2RX and
in Australia by Pluto Press Limited,
PO Box 199, Leichhardt, New South Wales 2040, Australia

Photoset by Colset Ltd, Singapore

Printed in Great Britain by Cox & Wyman Limited, Reading

Cover illustration by Paul Leith

ISBN 0 7453 0011 1

For Johnny

Brabt is a small, independent state on the coast between Holland and Belgium. There are one hundred and fifty gelds to the pound sterling, and, in 1981, eighty to the US dollar.

Contents

PART ONE: EXPOSITION

1

On the third Sunday of every month Commissioner Jan Argand visits his schizoparanoid wife in Hearts Haven, a private home some thirty kilometres south of the City of Brabt. On his visit in May 1981 he parked his car and picked his way up gravel paths and across lawns with just a little less sense of gloom than he usually does. The weather was fine; he knew his wife would be sitting out in one of the tiny sunhouses that dot the grounds, and for once he had something to talk about, something that would help get him through an always tedious and often horribly uncomfortable sixty minutes.

He found her in a small open gazebo set amongst laurels. She was on her own, sitting at a white cast-iron table which was littered with daisies. He stood in front of her and, as often happens at this moment, their eyes met – cold, knowing, blank, connecting between them a force-field of uncontaminated hate. Then he stooped to place his mouth an inch from her ear in a gestured embrace, swung another chair into the table, and sat beside her.

'You look well.'

She did not. In the last six months the complex of drugs Dr Liszt treated her with, each countering the side-effects of the other, had forced back incipient Parkinsonism but left her grossly obese, with grey, clammy skin. She had always been large, only briefly in the bloom of late adolescence attractive, now she was instantly repulsive.

3

'What are you doing?'

Maria Argand brusquely swept fifty or so of the tiny flowers to the ground. 'Sorting out the Fairy Queen's jewellery box?'

He knew from the questioning inflection that she was being sardonic, deliberately guying the more bizarre symptoms of her illness. Inwardly he sighed. In the early days he had welcomed such signs of a returning grip on reality, but recently he had come to admit to himself that he preferred her docile, drugged, bovine.

'I remember,' he said, rather hopelessly, 'my mother once tried to teach me to make daisy chains. But my father was angry, said it was not a suitable thing for a boy to be doing.'

Their eyes met again. The contempt in hers became yet sharper and it was his that flinched away first. Almost shyly he now put a large strong hand over her fat white one and thus they sat for a minute or so, each acutely embarrassed by the other's company, and even more by these tiny gestures that recognised that once a sort of affection had existed between them.

Argand is a heavily built man, but has not, like most of us of his age and position, allowed himself to get overweight. He has a grey melancholic face with high arched eyebrows and a large nose, which together might have been Punch-like had not the deep grooves on either side of his mouth given him an unrelentingly sombre look. For Sunday he was dressed in a tweed jacket over a fine-knitted roll-top sweater, with brown well-pressed trousers and shoes that shone like mirrors. He is obsessive about such things – after thirty-five years as a policeman he knows too much about the muck, the untidiness, the litter that surrounds and infiltrates our lives: to protect himself from it, he has built a shell of meticulous neatness about himself, a pattern of habits he hates to see disarranged. All this lies far more than he is willing to admit

4

behind his wife's withdrawal or escape into madness: but that he is the main cause of her illness he does concede, and for that reason gives up a very substantial proportion of his salary to keep her in Hearts Haven.

'Well,' he said, injecting forced brightness into his voice, 'I have some news.'

This was sufficient excuse for her to withdraw her hand. As he went on, she began to destroy daisy heads, petal by petal, holding them close to her face as she did so.

'On Friday I was called to the Maria Teresa Palace. You know, the headquarters of the Christian Democrat Party. Secretary Prinz was there. And Count Frederick, the Grand Duke's uncle.'

'I thought the Prince of Wales was going to marry our Duke's daughter.'

'Apparently not.' Argand is no longer disconcerted by non sequiturs of this sort, has trained himself to be relentlessly civil.

She did not look up from her daisies. 'Just as well,' she said with knowing satisfaction.

After a short silence Argand went on.

'There is to be a new bureau. They want me to head it. Its job will be to investigate complaints against the police. There have been rather a lot recently. Oh, I expect most of them are malicious . . . but the public deserves to feel that . . . things are by and large still done in the . . . right way.'

He shifted uneasily on the uncomfortable chair.

'Of course it won't be pleasant work. Looking into what is really one's colleagues' business. But at least it will be work.'

For six months, since Argand's return from the Virtue Islands, where he had been seconded to advise on the internal security of the new American base, Secretary Prinz had kept him busy enough on committees, working parties, even attending seminars and conferences on IS as far away as

Stockholm and Philadelphia. But it had not been work; not what Jan Argand called work.

'I don't think I would have accepted if . . . if I hadn't . . .' He couldn't find the words to express what he wanted to say, though it was simple enough. He would not have accepted had not boredom and lack of purpose become a quite serious problem which he lacked resources to cope with.

His wife, still without looking up, asked, 'What's this new bureau for?'

Still civil, he answered, 'To investigate complaints against the police.'

'No, but what is it *for?*'

He suppressed another sigh, looked out over the lawns. A peaceful scene – rose gardens near the house, buds on the point, swallows. A glass door in the orangery banged and a naked man, white hair, thin legs, leapt down stone mossy steps, sprinted over grass towards a high, glass-topped wall. Two men in pale blue overalls charged after him. It was all over in a moment: he was caught, and led back up into the house. Argand could hear him expostulating, protesting, and the soothing chat of the male nurses.

'What is it *for?*'

Well, *The Brabanter* had asked the same question and answered it by linking the new bureau with several other measures recently announced by the government – a freeze on metro fares, a commission to examine the feasibility of legalising pot, legislation to enforce workers' representation on the boards of public companies. All, said *The Brabanter* (a deeply conservative paper, which Argand read religiously), were cosmetic attempts to patch up the ruling coalition between the PBDC and the Reformed Socialist Party. Recent polls had suggested that in an election the Reformed Socialists would win more seats than the PBDC. The Moot still had three years to run but there was the danger that

6

Walter Beck, the new charismatic leader of the socialists, might bring down the coalition and force an early election . . . *The Brabanter*'s leader had been scornful, accused the PBDC of giving in to blackmail. The proper thing to do was to drop the socialists from the coalition and bring in the parties of the right. All of which aggravated Argand's already ambivalent feelings about his new post.

'What's it for? Why, to give me something to do, stop me from being a nuisance. That's what it's for.'

'Ha!' It was more a bark than a laugh, signified contempt rather than amusement.

The silence lengthened between them. Presently the new Commissioner for the Bureau of Advice and Investigation raked four or five wilted daisy heads over to his side of the table, and, like his demented wife, began methodically, one by one, to pull off the tiny petals. These he laid in neat rows, five to a row. Somewhere a blackbird sang.

2

August at Brichtzee was hot and sunny, the North Sea green then blue, the wind from the east blowing off the land, the beaches sheltered. In the middle of the promenade, the ostentatious hotels, built in imitation of Cannes and Nice, contrived to look quite splendid, and further out, where no one attempted to conceal the collapse of the town as a watering place, their poorer cousins looked brighter for a lick of sun even where paint was lacking.

Not a bad place to be, thought Detective Ensign Brian Tremp as he sauntered away from the casino towards the less fashionable, northern end of the front. That is, he tried to saunter, but it went against the grain – he was a smallish, neat, dapper sort of a man dressed with style and against the trend in neat Italian flannels, a French shirt, chrome-framed shades. His hair was close-cropped but layered, his feet twinkled in two-tone, open work shoes. Against the trend, for the Brabanters have many virtues and a few vices, but no one has ever praised them for or accused them of stylishness.

Which did not bother Tremp, though the realisation that he was not only stylishly dressed but dressed did catch him in the diaphragm as he discovered that there were more naked people around him than otherwise – not only on the shingle and sand below the sea wall but walking along the promenade or even just lying on it. From the neck down, most of the bodies he saw, both male and female, were instantly attractive – lean, tanned, young. Above the neck, which was usually hung with shells or beads, regardless of sex, less so – to Tremp anyway. Long, unkempt salt-filled hair; straggly moustaches above untrimmed beards on the men, and, now he allowed himself to look more closely, none of them noticeably clean. A whiff of marijuana passed beneath his nostrils, and involuntarily the strong expression his face had assumed shifted into a snarl.

Suddenly he was jostled – and since he knew about such things he recognised that it was no accident. Instinctively his left hand moved to his hip pocket to check – not a gun, he normally chose to be unarmed, but the leather folder with his warrant card. Then his right shoulder was caught too and he was turned through thirty degrees to face a youth who was tall, very blond, long-haired, deeply tanned. Tremp looked up into blue eyes and then compulsively at a small uncircumcised penis perched incongruously above a rather large scrotum. He felt rather than saw the presence of at least two other men, and a girl or two as well, crowding in.

'We don't go much for your sort here.'

'Come to gawp at our bums and tits, have you?'

'Or at bums and pricks. He looks the sort.'

'Why don't you take your clothes off and let us have a look.'

Tremp kept his head. He explained quietly that he was there on business to see Licentiate Nik Petersen at the Hotel Bristol.

'What business?'

Now Tremp did produce his warrant card – a new one, specially prepared for operatives of the Bureau of Advice and Investigation.

The tall bearded man was not Licentiate Petersen – but knew where to find him. Tremp was taken by five or six naked people across the main seafront road, through an

9

almost deserted public garden, rather seedy and rundown, and so into what had once been a medium-sized hotel of the sort patronised by the shopkeepers and clerks who now trudge up the Ordesa Valley or windsurf off Istria. Outside, the once-grand entrance had been daubed with a red device – '2LM' set in a circle; inside, most of the furniture had gone, packing cases and camping chairs serving instead. The dining room thus had a more spacious air than when forty or so families had sat down to long summer evening meals whose traditional ingredients were mainly sausage, potato, onion and eel. A trio had tinkled out sedate little waltzes and bacarolles in the background.

The piano – a white baby grand – remained. Licentiate Petersen sat behind it and was playing sturdier stuff, something noisy that Tremp knew must be classical. As the little procession approached, the music hesitated, paused, and switched to 'The International', played in ragtime.

Petersen was a big man, naked like the others, but fat, his brick-red skin covered with crisp yellow hair. A hearth-brush-sized moustache covered a large mouth above a small chin; his eyes behind round spectacles were pale blue and watery. A tall and quite beautiful girl had been sitting beside and behind him as he played, and now, as they both stood, Petersen laid a large left hand firmly over one of her buttocks – with his right he shook Tremp's hand.

When Tremp came to make his report, he omitted much of this, but filled in a few lines of biography on the complainant. Petersen was a lecturer in jurisprudence at Brabt University. He had often been in trouble with the authorities there but, through his popularity with the students and his clever manipulation of the statutes, had so far held on to his post. His skill as a lawyer was now deployed on behalf of the young people, a cell of the League of Marxist–Leninist Militants, who, he claimed, were being severely harassed by the police.

'First,' Petersen began, once they were sitting facing each other across a trestle table constructed from old planks in what had been the lounge, 'I must insist that this is not an illegal squat. The children are here with the acquiescence of the owners, who have accepted a sum of six thousand gelds as a deposit against damage. They therefore have precisely the same rights and protection against unwarranted search as any other Brabanter in the state from the Grand Duke down. Or up.' Yet, he explained, the police had broken in on three separate occasions, private property had been seized and three boys and one girl had been held in custody for twenty hours longer than was legal without an examining magistrate's warrant. On the third occasion, the police had not been the Rural Guards in whose jurisdiction they were, but the State Security Police. This time, no arrests had been made, and no drugs found either, because Petersen had told the children to clear them all out. Nevertheless, books and papers had been confiscated and two boys who tried to resist were swiftly and painfully beaten. One had suffered severe headaches ever since.

Tremp pointed out to Petersen, as he later did to Commissioner Argand in his report, that the occupants, squatters or not, had broken the law in a number of ways, from indecent exposure to smoking pot, that the police clearly had reasonable grounds for supposing that more serious offences had been committed, and it was their duty to investigate.

'Come, come.' Petersen absentmindedly scratched at his pubic hair. 'You must know that naked bathing is now permitted by popular consent at the extremities of public beaches. And it is policy to prosecute only those who deal in marijuana. It is nearly five years since anyone was done merely for possession.'

'But there is evidence of traffic,' Tremp insisted. 'One hundred grams were found in one place.'

Petersen sighed. 'This will be difficult for you to understand. We are a commune. All property is held in common. The children have pooled all they came with. Thus all the marijuana on the premises was in one place, all the money in another, and so on. When one needs something, one helps oneself to what one needs, and no more.'

Tremp shifted to the third raid. He had already been briefed on the background. At the end of the month a huge international demonstration was to take place at The Hok, the experimental nuclear power and research station and reprocessing plant up the coast at the mouth of the River Flot, and what State Security most feared was that extremist elements would attempt to penetrate the perimeter. They knew that several members of the Hotel Bristol Commune were activists in the anti-nuke campaign and had organised civil disobedience against nukes in the past. Particularly, they were concerned about three recent arrivals at the commune who might possibly be connected with the terrorist group Red Spectre, and they had raided the place looking for any material which might indicate what sort of actual risk The Hok was open to. Amongst much that was relevant they had found a detailed map of the installations, and there was no legitimate reason for it to be there.

As to the beatings, the State Security chief had had this to say: 'It's not a bad thing when these things happen. Those who see them are angry, they vow vengeance, but secretly they are frightened. They do not want the same to happen to them. And those who actually suffer do not want it to happen again. It works.'

But now Tremp had to admit the force of Licentiate Petersen's arguments. The law lecturer spoke briefly and to the point – clearly the unprepossessing appearance, the folds of patchily sunburnt skin, the continuous picking and scratching with chewed-down nails at most of the declivities

12

and orifices of his podgy body, concealed both intellect and determination.

If the students had broken laws, he argued, so undoubtedly had the police. According to the letter of the law, an examining magistrate should have issued warrants before they entered the hotel; it was even arguable that the students should have been given notice of this with the right to present arguments why warrants should not be issued. The beatings too clearly went beyond what was necessary for the police to complete their search, and were meant to intimidate through pain.

At the end of it all, Tremp left the Hotel Bristol in a confused state of mind, and later his report was confused too. The trouble was that the job itself was shot through with contradictions: it simply was not fair to ask a bright young policeman, ambitious and conscientious, to spend his time investigating complaints against his colleagues. As he walked away down the promenade, back into the normal everyday world of ice-creams, bikinis and bermuda shorts, where everything was properly regulated, he shook his head for the hundredth time at the absurdity of a bureau set up to investigate complaints against the police – and the double absurdity that he should have been seconded to it.

3

The City of Brabt, eighty kilometres from Brichtzee though only twenty from the sea, sited at the point where the River Flot ceases to be tidal, was a less pleasant place. The wind there was hot, trapped often into eddies of dust and ice-cream wrappers, smirched with petrol fumes. Most of the shops were shut, their owners walking in the Pyrenees or swimming off naturist campsites on the Adriatic. The few cafés still open had put their prices up and the coachloads of elderly Americans and Japanese, brought to see the third-best collection of Rembrandts in the world and the two Vermeers in the art gallery, grumbled while the couriers pocketed their commissions.

Detective Ensign Focking consulted his notebook once again, found the alley off Victoriastras he was looking for, and for a moment relished the cooler shade – though not the stale refuse nor the lean cats who scattered for shelter in front of him.

He was a large man running to fat and he sweated easily. As he panted up the open staircase to the apartment he was looking for he dabbed his forehead, lifted his shirt from his back, wriggled heavy toes in his open-ended leather sandals. The building was very old, its shell probably late medieval, though otherwise rebuilt and renovated once a century ever since. The sort of place that should have been torn down years ago, thought Focking, but cranks who like history campaign for preservation orders and the authorities them-

14

selves have found it useful to leave the area alone. It's Brabt's naughty square mile, with shady discos, drug dealers and hideouts for occasional terrorists on the run from Germany or further afield: it's handy to know where the villains can be found, or at any rate the scum who work for the villains.

Focking viewed his mission with a sense of quite powerful distaste, even stronger than Tremp's in Brichtzee, for it was not to one of the brightly painted doors hung with red, orange or green net curtains, with exotic if cheap oriental lamps, that he was climbing: prostitutes rarely have cause to complain about the police, the relationship is always symbiotic. But queers, perverts, are another matter . . .

He rang the bell on a plain attic door at the top, gritted his teeth for a moment, then recomposed his features. When the lean dark youth, not much more than a boy, opened the door, he saw a thick-set, red-faced man with a blond moustache and an expression which announced only the most open sort of bonhomie.

At first, Mik was nervous with Detective Ensign Piet Focking, but the latter's warm, bluff, no-nonsense manner, his readiness to have a lager, the way he admired their efforts to make the drab place more cheerful (tasselled lampshades, painted silk cushions) went a long way to setting him at ease. Mik explained that it was not he who had made the complaint, but his friend Paul – though, yes, it was he, Mik, who had been beaten. Paul was out at the shop getting their lunch, he would be back directly. Mik laughed uneasily, added in explanation that it was their one day off in the week, when the Aureole bar where they both worked was closed, and as usual they had forgotten to buy anything. Focking helped himself to a second beer, and noticed a shelf of cheap cookery books set between two rather obscene glass poodles – one was a bitch apparently on heat, the other a dog interested. The books, Mik explained, were Paul's. One day he hoped to be a chef.

15

Heavy steps outside, a click of the lock, and Paul came in – stocky, fair, moustached, quite the antithesis of Mik; though no one could seriously have taken them for brothers, Paul could well enough have been related to Focking. Once he knew who the policeman was and why he was there, he sat himself down with denimed knees spread, hands placed squarely on them, and leaned across the low glass-topped table.

'Last Friday night,' he said, 'three regular customers, friends of ours, are in the Aureole. One a student, the other two work in a record and cassette shop. Just before we close, two uniformed police, Public Order, come in as if just off their beat, sit down at the bar. Mik tells them one drink only, we are about to close. Then Mik asks these friends if they want to come up here for a schnapps and a game of cards, listen to records. Sometimes at the weekend they do that, sometimes they don't; last Friday they didn't. Mik closes up the bar, asks the policemen to leave. I hang on in the kitchen, clearing up the last dirty dishes, laying out trays for the morning breakfasts. When I come out, I hear a scuffling and a cry from the alley and I recognise Mik's voice. Mik, tell Detective Ensign Focking what happened.'

Mik shuddered, rolled despairing brown eyes at Paul, grimaced.

'Go on. The police were waiting for you outside. Is that right?'

'Yes, Paul.'

'And they bundled you up the alley. What happened then?'

'They hit me, Paul.'

'Until you were on your knees, yes?'

Focking leaned forward, eyes now very serious, but full of sympathy. He wiped beer suds from his moustache and said in a voice of well-modulated unctuousness, 'Mik. Don't be afraid. Tell it your way.'

16

Paul leaned back. 'Yes. That's right, Mik. You tell it your way.'

A fly buzzed out of the sparkling little kitchenette. Paul expertly slashed the air with a magazine, the insect toppled, still twitching, on to the glass-topped table. Almost tenderly, the kitchen hand from the Aureole bar picked it up by one wing, stood, walked to the window, and dropped it to float down five storeys to the area below. Then he sat down again.

'Go on, Mik. Tell him.'

'They hit me until I was on my knees.'

'Then they kicked you.'

'Then they kicked me.'

'In the balls.'

'Yes.'

Paul turned to Focking and nodded brusquely as if to say, there – what did I tell you.

'What did they say, Mik?'

'They said I had been . . . you know, soliciting, when I asked David and Jan and Bert to come up.'

'Yes?'

'And . . . do I have to say what else they said?'

'Yes, Mik, you do.'

Focking leaned forward again. 'Yes please, Mik. Tell it all. Just as it happened.'

'They said that soliciting was against the law.'

'Which,' said Focking, 'it is. For homosexuals.'

They both looked at him, eyes suddenly serious, wary, in Mik's case frightened.

'But they are friends. They play Belote with us and drink schnapps. Nothing else.'

'I know,' said the Detective Ensign. 'You said. Go on.'

'Well. The police said I had broken the law. But that it wasn't worth making a case of it, so they were just roughing me up to make sure I didn't do it again.'

'Then what, Mik?'

'That was all, Paul. Then you came.'

'No. Before that, what did they say?'

'Oh yes.' Thus prompted, Mik spoke quickly. 'They said it wouldn't be long before all of us . . . people like us . . .'

'Homosexuals.' Focking dropped the word in again, like a stone.

'Yes. Would be rounded up and herded away. That we are deviants, and corrupt, and . . . oh, all that sort of thing, they said, but that times . . .'

'Times are going to change.'

'That's right, Paul. That things are changing and we would have to change too or else we would be put away, like the Jews were, and the people like us then too, in the war. You know?'

Focking nodded slowly. 'I know,' he said.

'They said a time of moral regeneration was coming.'

4

'Nik.'

'Lisa.'

'Stop playing for a moment.'

'Is it so bad?'

'No, of course not. But there's something important.'

Licentiate Petersen lifted his heavy hands from the keyboard and placed them on the glossy white top of the baby grand. There, to Lisa standing above them, they looked like nothing so much as red sausages on a butcher's slab.

'What is it?'

Red face on one side, eyes behind his spectacles serious. Really though, he is much too fat. It won't do. She recollected herself. 'It's Wilhelm. Margarethe and the others are worried about him.'

'Head still aches?'

'Not just that. He's still asleep and they don't like the way he looks.'

Petersen glanced at his watch, nestling in almost white hairs on his thick wrist. 'It's eleven o'clock now. When was he last awake?'

'I don't know. Last night. Late yesterday evening.'

'I'll come and see.'

The big man lurched down the step off the platform – once, no doubt, it had been framed in ferns, banked with hydrangeas – and padded across the wide, cool twilit dining room. Lisa, tall, blonde, wide-hipped, drifted behind him into the foyer, to the foot of the stairs. They both wore sandals, beads, wristwatches, nothing else.

'He's on the second floor,' she said.

Petersen was quite badly out of breath by the time they reached the landing and he had to wait for half a minute, holding on to the wrought-iron and brass banister.

'Room 212, on the left.'

It overlooked the sea, had a balcony with a stuccoed balustrade, was consequently light and airy. The heavy embossed wallpaper had begun to fall, so the occupants, two of Petersen's students, had ripped off as much of it as they could, leaving pale pink blotchy plaster exposed. On this they had hung posters – against whaling and nuclear technology, for 2LM, Rosa Luxembourg.

There were airbeds on the floor, two or three plastic bags, a rucksack. Wilhelm, a tall, dark youth, lay twisted half on his back beneath a single coarse blanket; his face had the waxy, dirty pallor of a dead fish. A boy and a girl stood as Petersen came in, and a third joined them from down the corridor.

Petersen got on to one knee, stooped, managed to place his ear somewhere near Wilhelm's mouth and chest. He stayed quite still, motioned the others to be quiet, then straightened.

'He's in a bad way. Very bad. Hardly breathing and the air sounds in his windpipe.'

The girl, Margarethe, began to weep quite loudly, gasping, between sobs, 'What can we do, what can we do?' She had lank, mousy hair and a pallid, long-waisted body, slightly pot-bellied – an Eve by Van Eyck.

Petersen spoke quickly to the oldest of the youths, the one who had first spoken to Tremp on the seafront. 'Jan, go to my room. Take money off the mantel-shelf. Then go to the nearest phone and get an ambulance.'

* * *

Inevitably, there were delays. The nearest working public phone was in a café three buildings away. The owner, a large, strong lady, would not allow Jan in with no clothes on, laughed when he said his friend was dying, and drove him out with a mop. Back in jeans and a sweatshirt, he at last got through to the first ambulance firm listed on the back of the booth, but when he gave the address – Hotel Bristol – he was told curtly that nothing was doing. Ambulance firms in Brabt expect to be paid on the spot and it is up to the patient to reclaim the fee later from social security. The minimum is five thousand gelds, a sum quite probably in excess of what a nudist anarchist squatter might be expected to have on his person. The second firm was more sympathetic: there would be a vehicle on its way immediately – they were in radio contact with one patrolling near the town centre.

At Brichtzee general hospital there were further hold-ups. The only doctor on duty was removing a fish-hook from a small girl's foot. Petersen, in check shirt now, jeans, with a broad leather belt slung below his paunch, lost his temper, stamped about the low-ceilinged reception area, pushed trolleys out of his way, abused the nurses. The doctor bent over the girl's foot, determined to be as neat and thorough as possible. The girl whimpered; he squirted the lesion with combined disinfectant and painkiller. Then, with special pliers (for fish-hook extraction is a common enough affair by the seaside), he snipped off the eye with its knot of nylon line and was able to ease the hook round in a semi-circle, going with the barb, not against it, and so bring it out through a fresh exit wound. It chinked in the enamel kidney dish at his elbow.

'I have a friend out here, nearly dead,' bellowed Petersen, pulling back the cubicle curtain. 'Will you come?'

Angry retorts came to the doctor's lips, but behind Petersen the casualty sister appeared – she looked worried too, very worried.

Within minutes, Wilhelm was plugged into mobile life-support and monitoring systems, and the lot – a load of machinery with a near-corpse at the centre of it – was wheeled off to X-ray. Petersen stamped about behind the technicians, his leather sandals slapping on the polished vinyl floors. 'It's typical,' he cried. 'Always the same. You come in naked and near-dead and no one cares, but dress in a nice clean frock, with a scratch on your foot, and all the wonders of modern science are . . .'

The doctor hit him. Not hard, but noisily, on the cheek. 'Tell me how this boy came to be like this.'

Shocked, and suddenly humble too, Petersen pulled himself together.

'He was beaten. Eight days ago. About the head with truncheons, blackjacks. By the filth. He's been bad since, and then this morning he was like this.'

The doctor was suddenly very angry indeed. 'Eight days,' he hissed. 'Eight days.'

'But he did not complain,' wailed Petersen as the quietly jangling procession slid away across black floors, beneath the strip lighting, through heavy plastic doors that flapped to behind them.

Margarethe plucked at Petersen's sleeve.

'Will he be all right?'

Petersen massaged his still-stinging cheek.

'Perhaps. Perhaps. We can only hope. But he looked as good as gone to me, he really did. As good as gone.'

5

He was right. But it was not until ten o'clock that night that the doctors and surgeons finally decided that Wilhelm Koonig was irrecuperable; that is, it was then they disconnected him from the machinery of which he had never been more than the least efficient part, removed his undamaged kidneys, which would be found a home elsewhere in the hospital, and wrote out in treble quintuplicate that he had become clinically dead. Thus it was not until he reached his office next morning that Argand heard of it.

Two hours earlier he had woken up in his new apartment near the top of a modern block four kilometres from the centre of Brabt. He had moved there on his return from the Virtue Islands. He was still convalescent from mental illness and his old flat had suddenly seemed horrible to him. Dr Liszt had recommended a clean break with the past and Argand had followed his advice – an expert himself, he believed in experts. Especially, he believed in the expert who was prepared to keep his wife in Hearts Haven.

At first, he had hated the change: the clean pastel colours after ochres and browns; the light modern furniture after the heavy old stuff that had seemed so grand when his parents gave it to him on his wedding day in 1948; the modern appliances which so far had worked perfectly – the fridge which did not defrost if you put frozen food in it, the hot water that was always just right, never scalded nor ran cold.

He had hated it all because unconsciously he presumed that his wife would have loved it, and so he felt guilty that he was enjoying it and she was not. Then, one third Sunday, she had suddenly said, quite lucidly, 'You should get out of that old apartment – it's like an undertaker's parlour.'

He had not been able to tell her that he already had, but next morning, as he stood at the high window, sixteen storeys up and looked out over the city of Brabt – its medieval quarter round Victoriastras, the government offices on Wilhelmstras, the smart boulevards leading down to the River Flot, Wilhelmspark and the hill rising to the fairy-tale castle built in 1870 – he had felt a tension slip out of his shoulders and his back, had decided that perhaps Dr Liszt was right, that this was a better place to be. And to shave in water precisely the temperature he wanted it to be was, after all, pleasant.

But other habits died hard. The Louis Bonaparte was still on his route to work, though now to reach it required ten minutes in a bus rather than a five-minute walk; and the newspaper kiosk where he had always bought his daily copy of *The Brabanter* was just by the bus stop. Thus, that day, as on every other working day since his wife went into Hearts Haven, he was, at half past eight in the morning, drinking coffee and breaking one of the small, warm, slightly sweet loaves that old-fashioned Brabanters have for their breakfast. He still muttered, though not quite remembering why, over the foil-wrapped butter (once it had been crumbly, moist, sliced from a block *en motte*), as he scanned the headlines.

'Beck to Attend The Hok Plant Protest' ran second to Brezhnev at the Polish Communist Party's Congress in Warsaw. Not caring too much what evil men with evil beliefs were up to on the other side of the Iron Curtain, Argand read the report on Beck. He suspected Beck was an evil man – though, because Argand was a Brabanter, and many solid, sensible Brabanters had found a good word or two to say for Beck, he was prepared for the time being to suspend judgement. The new leader of the Reformed Socialists had reaffirmed his support for his party's official policy of a two-year moratorium on all nuclear projects – whether for energy or defence: this to include the refusal to site Cruise and Pershing missiles on Brabanter soil, and the progressive closing-down of the reactor at The Hok. 'I shall certainly attend The Hok International Rally,' Beck had announced in a press conference called at party headquarters, 'and if the organisers wish me to speak there I shall be happy to do so.'

The organisers were welcoming, enthusiastic. 'Of course there will be speeches,' a spokesperson had said, 'and so of course there will be an opportunity for Deputy Prime Minister Beck to speak.'

Argand turned to the middle-page leader. 'If Beck is about to campaign publicly on an issue in opposition to PBDC policy, then he cannot expect to remain part of the coalition for much longer. Whether or not his party as a whole is behind him, or simply the extreme left-wing, who so crudely manipulated the anti-nuclear vote at last month's conference, remains to be seen, but we venture to suggest that the shrewd and practical people of Brabt will reject a policy that is likely to leave their electricity cut off for twelve hours in every twenty-four . . .'

Argand, nodding in warm agreement, read on to the second leader. This condemned the appointment of Catedratika Julia Arendt as Dean of the Arts Faculty. This, like other recent measures, was clearly a political move designed to win back liberals to the PBDC. But Arendt was no liberal – she was a Marxist, and a feminist. To seek votes by such measures shows the level to which standards in public life had sunk.

As indeed had those of the Louis Bonaparte: Argand

crumpled the butter foil into the tiny plastic tub from which he had scooped a teaspoonful of plum jam, and looked around for his bill. It was there instantly – whatever else had gone, a sound respect for a loyal customer remained.

He hated his new office, which was in the basement of a tower block whose principal occupant was a state-owned bank. In contrast to his new flat, the modernity here was pretentious rather than functional. But his new secretary was a different matter altogether. Dm Petra Madjen was a thin, grey woman, a spinster, devoted to the dour Jansenist strain of Catholicism that is typical of Brabt, and relentlessly efficient. She was small too, and about the same age as Maria Argand but as different as possible in every other way – in short, wholly acceptable. Not that Argand ever consciously made the comparison. It was enough that in her presence he felt secure, reassured, unthreatened: for him, a rare enough experience where women are concerned.

It was not her fault that the news she brought was bad. Secretary Prinz had phoned from his home to say he would be over by ten o'clock. Argand's feelings about Prinz were confused. He respected his family connection with the Grand Dukes, his polish, his upper-class ease, the fact that he had represented Brabt at the Helsinki Olympics on the back of a horse, that he was the senior Brabanter executive for Internal Affairs. As such, he was directly responsible for seeing that cabinet decisions were carried out – he had survived in that post through four PBDC-led coalitions, and now cabinets tended to listen to him rather than command.

On the other hand, he disliked Prinz's bonhomie, suspected him generally of bad faith, knew for sure that once at least his own life had been held cheap by the Secretary. Above all, or rather in front of all, for it was always the first thing to impinge on Argand, he hated Prinz's pipe.

Yet the Commissioner's deeply rooted faith in order, hierarchy, the rightness of things as they are and the people who maintain them so, mitigated all. Prinz was his superior, the man he was answerable to, the man who had ordered the creation of the Bureau of Advice and Investigation and had appointed Argand its Commissioner. But the depression remained – it was bad news when Prinz called on his subordinates instead of summoning them, a sign that he was about to ask of them something that they would not readily agree to. Vaguely, Argand wondered if it were to do with Beck's decision to attend the rally at The Hok.

But the news Prinz brought, once the pipe smoke was swirling round his head, and his large bottom, loosely and flatteringly clad in English-cut trousers, had been parked on the Commissioner's desk, was of Wilhelm Koonig's death the night before, at Brichtzee general hospital.

'Of course, you see the difficulty, Jan.' The pipe was removed, the drooping moist lip gently dabbed, the pipe replaced. 'Your people are already investigating the Hotel Bristol raids, and we can be sure Licentiate Petersen is going to make the most of this. The radical press too will make a test case out of it, judge the efficacy, even the genuineness, of the exercise you are engaged in. Are you with me? Quite. Well. First things first. Do you have any preliminary report? I mean, has your man put anything in writing yet?'

Argand pulled Tremp's report out of the pile of folders at the right-hand end of the desk and passed it up. Prinz leafed it open, saw that there was more than one page of A4 and let it drop.

'Give me the gist,' he said.

Argand described the raids and concluded, 'By common current practice, the police did nothing unusual, nothing that in practical terms was not justifiable. They acted according to the evidence they had in the sort of way that is

27

now judged to be the most expedient; nevertheless, it is undeniable that they broke the law and Ministry Standing Orders. Therefore, reluctantly, I am about to advise the Brichtzee examining magistrate to proceed.' He frowned, aware that he had added his own bias to Tremp's. In fact, the police were more culpable than he had implied, and he knew it.

Prinz, however, beamed. 'I think on the whole that's good news, though it would look better still if you had already sent the file to Justice Vustouk. You see, the Frenchman in the potato field' – he used a popular but spurious 'peasant' proverb – 'is Licentiate Petersen. He made the first complaint, he'll now have to maintain his position, his reputation, by pressing as hard as he can. You see, he plans to stand in one of the newer marginal suburbs and this affair is going to be important to him.'

He hitched himself off the desk, sucked flame from his gold lighter into his pipe and peered up through smoke at the legs of pedestrians on the pavement outside. Two young girls went by. 'Nice view. Well, I tell you what I think. I think we must be punctilious and meticulous about the procedures indicated. Pre-empt any reproach Petersen might throw at us. What do you think, Jan?'

Argand looked up from the blotter where he had been doodling an abstract but jagged and heavily shaded pattern.

'It had never occurred to me that any other course of action is open to us.'

If Prinz was aware of sarcasm, he did not show it.

'That's fine then. And this man Tremp.' He tapped the folder. 'Is he up to it?'

'I think so.'

'Well, leave him on it since he already knows the background, but keep an eye on him and back him up. I'm sure the best way to deal with this is to have a State Security

Trooper locked up on remand as soon as possible, no matter what Commissioner General Gapp might say, then it'll all fade away. We can always get the poor chap off the hook later on in the day if need be.'

6

'You have lodged a complaint against the police with this new bureau of advice and consent or whatever.' The owner of the Aureole bar was checking the cash register, Paul and Mik looking on. Feeling a quick stab of fright in his diaphragm, Paul took a gulp from the tall stein of lager he had beside him. At the end of the day, the patron allowed them a litre each from the *presson*, though often they did not bother to take it.

'Well?'

'Well, yes.'

'Better if you dropped it.'

Silence fell over the little bar, lit now by only one bulb. The heavy glass doors had been pulled to and locked, the chairs placed on the tables, Space Invaders were silent and blank. It was a time Paul and Mik usually enjoyed – they got genuine satisfaction from the boss's weekly visit, his usual quiet approval of the way things had gone. They recognised his need to find some detail to grumble at – they would have judged him lacking in the qualities that make a good boss if he hadn't – but they knew they did their job well, knew he knew, and that was enough. The coins were all now neatly stacked in the amounts the bank liked to have them and the owner – a thin, dyspeptic man, nearly sixty, with a wooden leg won in the Resistance in 1944 and the ultimate source of his wealth – was wrapping them neatly and skilfully in strips of newspaper, folding the ends over each stack in turn.

'Better if you dropped it.'

Paul maintained a stubborn silence.

'Look. You know as well as I do a place like this, in a quarter like this, we have to have the police on our side. It's not possible, one way or another, that we don't break some God-cursed law five, six times a day. So drop it, OK?' He turned to Mik. 'The till is short eight gelds. So I stop your wages eight gelds, all right?' He always said this, but never carried out the threat.

'It's gone too far to stop,' said Paul. 'Too far. Anyway, it's nothing to do with you or the Aureole. It's a personal thing.'

The patron turned, head on one side, dark brown eyes separated by a nose the Gestapo had broken. 'So you want a hand-out too? You want me to pay you to drop this thing?'

'No. Of course not.'

'I am glad to hear that, because I would not pay you a single geld. Friends at the precinct police station are not easy to find, and once you have them you hold on. But kitchen hands . . . poof! Don't think I don't like you, don't think I don't know you give me a fair honest deal, and I hope I give you one back. But I can find a new kitchen hand as easy as I find potatoes in a potato field. Now think of that.' He lifted the counter flap and swung himself and his wooden leg across the wet floor Mik had just swabbed, then paused at the door, his hand on the self-locking catch. 'Mind you lock up well.' Another thing he always said. 'And mind they tell me down at the station tomorrow evening that you've dropped this thing – or else tomorrow is the last day you work for me.'

Paul was angry. His fair face had flushed at the accusation that he wanted money. An inner resentment too had flared like an irritated ulcer at the talk of fair deals all round – he knew the patron took four times his and Mik's combined wages out of the Aureole, which was by no means his only

31

business, and did little more in the way of work than pay the bills and bank the profit.

'We shan't drop it. We shan't,' he said. 'Will we, Mik?'

Mik, thin, dark, eyes like a frightened rabbit's, looked from one to the other and back again in helpless bewilderment.

The patron's normal pallor was more marked than ever, apart from a red spot on each cheek. 'Tomorrow evening. A different story, OK?' He pushed open the door, lurched through, let it swing shut behind him – and the locks clicked chunkily into place. Paul and Mik saw him swinging his way down the pavement, round the corner into Victoriastras.

Ten minutes later, they left together. They had said nothing at all to each other after the patron had gone, both knowing there was nothing to be said right away on the matter. Mik accepted that, after all, Paul was doing the right thing; Paul suspected that Mik's attitude, which was the same as the patron's, was the sensible, politic, expedient one. But, if sense and policy were what counted, then they would both still be living in the Zar, in the mines or allied work, and engaged or married to each other's sisters.

Near the top of the open staircase that led to their attic, three men were waiting for them. In the darkness it was difficult to be sure of anything, though later Paul and Mik agreed that the attackers had been heavy and strong, not youths, that all had been dressed alike in jeans and black leather jackets, that they were lean and hard, and had short or shortish hair. They hustled the two lads into the unlit apartment and then, while one boxed them into a corner of the tiny kitchen flourishing a short length of weighted hose which he swung to their ribs or thighs and once to Paul's face, the other two began methodically to break up everything they could find that could be broken.

They tore down the lampshades and trampled on them, ripped up Paul's cookery books, wrenched the silk-covered cushions apart, smashed all the glass and china, toppled the fridge and trampled the contents with heavy, military-looking boots. For a brief moment, the one with the weighted hose was dramatically lit from below by the light that came on in the refrigerator. Mik's wide frightened eyes took in little of the face, which remained largely in shadow except for a thin-lipped mouth drawn back in a snarl to reveal two gold molars. Then a lean arm reached out to close the fridge door, and extinguish the light, and, for less than a second, a tattoo on the man's forearm was partially uncovered as his cuff rode up – a scroll it looked like and the words in gothic script '. . . Hath No Man.'

They were done. To round off the sack of the apartment, one of them picked up the heavy glass poodles and let them drop, one after the other, to twist in moonlit freefall and shatter explosively in the area below.

When Paul withdrew his complaint, Argand sent Focking to find out why. Focking noted the still-wrecked flat and Paul's bruised face without comment. He listened to Paul's sullenly repeated refusal to give any answer, his obsessive insistence that the withdrawal of his complaint was his business only; there was no law or regulation that compelled him to say why he wanted to.

Focking nodded in solemn agreement. 'No law at all. And would I be right in thinking that, if the Commissioner decided after all to keep the file open, you would refuse to repeat the accusations?'

Paul looked up – his good eye widening, a pulse throbbing in the swollen lid of the other. 'He can't do that. Can't keep the file open.'

Focking grimaced, pulling down his bottom lip. 'Commissioners are a law unto themselves,' he said. He reached for his lager, wiped his moustache, and then smiled again with the frank openness that had won Mik's trust. 'But there wouldn't be much point, would there, if you're ready to say it was all a pack of lies, what you said the first time.' He stood up to go, patted Paul's shoulder, winked at Mik who had remained like a petrified rabbit in front of a stoat. 'No. I think you're right though. Best to forget all about it – silly incident, nothing to it, just one of those things, one gets over them. I'm sure you won't hear any more from us if we don't hear any more from you.'

In his report Focking declared that Paul had refused to make any coherent statement, but when asked if he had re-considered the justice of his complaint said yes, he had. Focking concluded with his own opinion: that the complain-ant had realised the weakness of his case – possibly he had expected the three youths his friend had been heard solic-iting to back his version and had found that they would not.

7

It was Argand's way never to move about the City of Brabt other than on foot, unless the distance to be covered made walking an absurdity. He often excused this idiosyncracy by saying that thus he kept in touch with the mood of the City – one of whose guardians he had been throughout his working life. This 'being in touch', vague though it was, was important, had helped when he had worked in the Bureau for the Prevention and Detection of Crime, and even more when he had been transferred to Public Order. He could – for he was after all now over fifty, and had reached the highest rank open to him, a rank which carried on formal occasions the honorific 'Excellency' – ramble on at some length on this subject, especially when addressing new recruits, or when stuck for something to say on the very rare occasions when he was asked out to dinner. The truth of the matter, which he would have been embarrassed to admit even to himself, was that he was more than a little in love with his City – a genuine emotion this, quite unlike that claimed by aldermen laying foundation stones or legislators using vandalism as an excuse for introducing new and repressive laws.

Thus, as he walked next day from his office under the Agricult Credit Tower to the Ministry of Internal Affairs, he took a slight detour through a pedestrian precinct that had Rinusplatz at its centre: really because he liked its baroque but small-scale perfection and the flowerstalls beneath the statue of Prince Rinus but telling himself that he wanted to see the Vigil of Witness reported in that morning's edition of *The Brabanter*.

The vigil turned out to be a round half-century, mainly women, mostly middle-aged, holding banners and placards. They looked rather sheepish, as if invisible pens kept them in place. According to the newspaper, they would remain there for a week, night and day: that is, always fifty people, neither more nor fewer, replacing each other in carefully ordered relays. Fifty, because that was the maximum the police would allow and because the organisers had declared it a matter of sacred principle that the force of their witness should never fall one jot below the maximum allowed.

With an expert eye for crowds and gatherings, the ex-Commissioner for Public Order quickly made the total only forty-eight, and was about to shake his head wisely at the presumption of people with sacred principles, when two stoutish housewives, loaded with string and plastic bags, trotted up. Muttering apologies to their colleagues, they put down their shopping and took up their crosses – for thus the placards were designed. One said CHRIST NOT MAMMON; the other LOVE NOT PORN. Argand began to read the rest – for all were different – and discovered that in many cases the religious content was a veneer for the covertly political. A MAN WHO IS WORTHY OF HIS HIRE NEEDS NO UNION; ABORTION: THE RIGHT OF WOMEN TO CHOOSE SATAN; and in one case a political message combined with an anti-semitic one: KARL MARX IS A WORTHY DESCENDANT OF THOSE WHO CRUCIFIED OUR LORD. There was a sort of skill in all this that he half admired (for, in so far as he allowed himself opinions on public matters – considering them on the whole improper luxuries for a servant of the state – there was little here he objected to except the anti-semitism), admired because he knew one of the conditions of this vigil was that the placards should not be political.

In the centre of it all a large banner proclaimed the immediate purpose: IF YOU AGREE WITH ANY, ALL, OR SOME OF WHAT WE STAND FOR COME TO THE FESTIVAL OF MORAL REGENERATION – BRABT CITY STADE, 15 AND 16 AUGUST.

Saturday and Sunday at the end of this week, Argand thought. He glanced at his watch and hurried on.

The Committee of Public Safety was a standing committee consisting of the six Commissioners of Police. The chair was usually taken by one of Secretary Prinz's deputies, but today he was there in person. Seated at, or rather spread across, the end of the rectangular table in the meeting room – with portraits of past officials on the walls behind them and lit by a small chandelier – Prinz, his smile that of a not quite honest Buddha, thumbed tobacco into the bowl of his pipe and opened the proceedings.

'According to our constitution, an extraordinary meeting to discuss a matter of vital interest to the safety of the state may be called if two of our members are agreed that a situation has arisen to warrant it. Excellency Wynand, Commissioner for the Rural Guard, has called this meeting, and he is seconded by Excellency General Gapp, Commissioner for State Security. Excellency Wynand.'

The gold lighter flared and Argand, sitting with the Commissioner for Traffic and Transport and the Commissioner for Public Order and opposite Crime, State Security and the Rural Guard, flinched away from the fumes.

Wynand, a small brisk man with a large mole on his right cheek and short stubby fingers that fidgeted on the blotter in front of him, began. He spoke quickly, in short staccato sentences that left the impression that what he was saying was well thought out and concisely put. In fact on this occasion, as on others, he was muddled.

'Chairman, Excellencies. The creation of the Bureau of Advice and Investigation is my reason for calling this meeting. Let me make clear that I intend no personal attack on the Excellent Commissioner in charge. He is a man we all hold in esteem. But what I aim to show is that this new bureau is not functioning in the interest of public safety. That there is no real reason for its existence. But, its existence granted, its constitution needs to be redrawn. Its powers limited. And I would propose that we recommend that its revised constitution is submitted to this committee for approval.'

At his elbow, General Gapp shifted slightly and his finger pointed to the notes Wynand had in front of him.

'And I would submit,' Wynand added, 'that a moratorium on the operation of the Bureau of Advice and Investigation be declared, until these steps have been taken.'

The rest of his remarks added up to little more than a summary of the Hotel Bristol case: how in his opinion his men in the first two raids had acted in exemplary fashion, how the investigation into their conduct, now apparently dropped, had caused much expense of time and money, how the raids were justified anyway by the discovery of cannabis and the lack of hygiene and the fire risks. Meanwhile, the morale of the men in the Brichtzee section of his force had suffered, and anyway it was well known that Licentiate Petersen had initiated the complaints to further his political ambitions. He concluded by saying that he felt sure the other Commissioners had found themselves similarly harassed and that Commissioner Argand too, with all his experience of the difficulties and hazards in two of the bureaus, would agree to the proposals he, Wynand, had put before them.

Prinz laid his pipe in the stained granite bowl at his elbow, where it continued to fume. A grunt cleared the phlegm from his throat.

'We have listened to Excellency Commissioner Wynand with interest and concern. Excellency Commissioner General Gapp has agreed to second the proposals we have just heard.' He picked up his pipe again, attempted to tap out stinking ashes, failed, delved in a waistcoat pocket for a pen-knife, with which he scraped out the recalcitrant cinders. At last he sat back, but with his pouch on his lap, again thumbing more tobacco into the bowl. 'Pray continue, General. Don't wait on my account,' and his smile was as bland as ever.

Gapp passed a mottled hand across his silvered blond hair, glanced sidelong at the Secretary, grimaced, then fixed his cold pale eyes on a point about a metre above Argand's right shoulder.

'Chairman, Excellencies. I second the Excellent Commissioner's proposals,' he began, 'and before I explain why I would like to return to the affair of the Hotel Bristol. As I expect you all know, the third raid on that unpleasant place was carried out by a section of the force I command and, following the death of one of the unfortunates who lived there, there is now in process an official and judicial inquiry into that raid. Now I have the utmost confidence that that inquiry will absolutely vindicate each and every action my men undertook there. I say this to impress upon your Excellencies that I come before you now not on account of that silly, farcical affair, but because in my mind the issues raised by the creation of the Bureau of Advice and Investigation should be considered on a much broader, more general plane, from a more philosophical point of view.'

Here Secretary Prinz appeared to sigh – his cadaver slowly inflated and then subsided again, but all done noiselessly.

'Our people, whom we serve, are divided, but unevenly so.

On the one side is the vast majority, the decent sorts, those with a positive, accepting, national consciousness, good people who accept not in words only but with every action of their lives the state and its ruling, constitutional order. They see and acknowledge the highest positive value in the constitution of our state, in whose service they spend their lives.

'On the other side' – Gapp's left hand took over from the right the job of tapping emphasis on his blotter – 'there is a tiny but vociferous and active minority who threaten the whole structure of our state and thus the lives of the majority who honour and serve it. They are ill disposed to the state, they have rejected it, they defame it, their ultimate aim is to subvert it. And in recent years, since the PBDC has been allied in coalition with the Socialists, the state itself has betrayed itself with an extended bout of libertarianism that has actually encouraged these dissidents, fostered their anti-social lifestyles, and permitted them to preach publicly policies which, if carried out, would bring about the very dissolution of the state.

'Too many concessions have been made. Too many sound laws, many of them ancient and traditional, have been repealed, and the net result, Excellencies, has been a growing impudence, a cockiness, even in the end a sort of pretension, amongst this tiny minority of dissidents of which I am speaking. All this, Excellencies, has made the work of my bureau increasingly onerous, has multiplied its extent enormously, for this presumption of which I speak has led to the deliberate creation of an opposing power over and against this state; it has led to the greatest blasphemy of all – the denial of the state's monopoly of violence.'

Here a sort of dry rasp came into Gapp's voice. He raised a clenched fist a few centimetres above the table, let it fall back, but gently, as if mindful at the last moment of where he was; then he raised the same hand and with his index finger flicked specks of spittle from each corner of his thin mouth.

'Excellencies, the concession in this bout of libertarianism which has given most comfort and support to these enemies of the state is the one we are considering today, the Bureau of Advice and Investigation, for it calls into question the whole nature of our function as policemen, it questions the very essence of what we are, of what we have been created to do. I honestly believe it will do more harm in the long run than even the Freedom of Information Bill Deputy Prime Minister Beck plans to introduce in the next session of the Moot.

'At this moment in time I fear this new bureau for a very particular reason. Your Excellencies are all aware that at the end of this month there is to be held, with the permission of the Minister of Internal Affairs, a massive demonstration against the nuclear power and research plant at The Hok. Many thousands, perhaps two hundred thousand, from all over Europe, of those disaffected of which I speak will attend. This is going to place a terrible strain on the resources of Commissioner Wynand's Rural Guard, on Commissioner Pranck's Public Order, an intolerable strain even if every single one of those disaffected dissidents acts for every moment of the demonstration without breaking the law.

'But that is not all. Amongst that quarter-million there will be many, perhaps a hundred or more, who are not just disaffected but are active members of groups like the Red Brigades, RAF, the IRA, ETA, and our own local variety, Red Spectre. These will not be content simply to jog their bodies about to popular music, smoke cannabis and assume thereby they are helping some obscurantist cause or other. What they will attempt is an act of sabotage on the nuclear reactor itself. It is because we suspect such an attempt is to be

41

made that we raided the Hotel Bristol, and there indeed we did find certain documents concerning The Hok demonstration. I do not need to tell you what the consequences of such an act of sabotage would be, if it were successful.

'A month ago I would have said it could not be successful. Then I had confidence in my force. Then I knew that, with the powers we have, and the internal discipline we command, any such attempt would have been forestalled. Now . . . I do not know. Why not? Because of this new bureau. How can my men follow up every lead, question every suspect, break up subversive groupings, confiscate subversive material, if at every turn they are going to be subject to proceedings brought by this new bureau?'

Stent, for Crime, a large, bluff man – efficient, but known to court publicity – abruptly raised his hand.

'Chairman. Point of order.'

Prinz nodded.

Stent continued, 'Surely it is the military's responsibility to guard all nuclear installations? And there is a detachment of the Mobile Operations Unit permanently based at The Hok?'

Gapp sighed. 'Yes, Stent. That is so. But only once the perimeter has been broken does MOBOP take over. It is the job of my bureau to forestall such an eventuality. May I continue?'

Prinz nodded again.

'I have enlarged after all on a particular case, that of the demonstration at The Hok. But let me conclude by returning to the general, overall philosophical view.

'It surely cannot be disputed that, of all the organs of the state, the one most immediately and forcibly confronted with reality is the police. We have uniquely privileged access to knowledge which enables us to understand a multiplicity and diversity of socially deviant and anti-social forms of

behaviour, structural defects in society and the laws govern-
ing social mass behaviour. To put this knowledge to its full
and proper use in the defence of the state, we should now be
transforming ourselves from a subordinate object with
merely executive functions into actual initiators of processes
which will actively benefit society and the state. But at this
crucial moment this Bureau of Advice and Investigation has
been set up, this new Freedom of Information Bill is
proposed, both restricting us more completely to our traditional functions than ever before. They should both be
resisted, swept away. And we must grasp a completely new
awareness of ourselves as the active and instituted guardians
and, where necessary, creators of social hygiene. Chairman,
Excellencies, I second Commissioner Wynand's proposals.'

At Brabt Stade, at the coming Festival of Moral Regeneration, this impassioned appeal (all the more impressive
because of the low-key delivery) would no doubt have
provoked stormy, hysterical applause. In the event there was
a speech that did, and very similar indeed it was to General
Gapp's in certain respects, phrasing and so on, and broadly
on the same subject: the role of the police in a threatened
state. But, in this particular committee room in the Ministry
of the Interior, Gapp's peroration simply intensified a dull,
hot silence. Deprived of the right to cheer, or jeer, his
audience of six sat in mute embarrassment, avoiding each
other's eyes, fiddling with pens, blotters, gazing at their
knees or the ceiling.

A sharp click and most eyes switched to Secretary Prinz,
who was slipping his gold-cased pen into his upper inside
pocket.

'Excellencies.' He smiled at all equally and beatifically. 'I
think I have understood the pertinent points of the Excellent
Commissioners' remarks and their proposals. Now. It would

be most improper of us to attempt to initiate here a process whereby cases now under consideration by the Bureau of Advice and Investigation were simply dropped. To do so would bring many thousands of General Gapp's tiny disaffected minority out on to the streets. At the same time, both proposer and seconder have raised very important issues, have given us much food for thought. I think we should, I think we must, give ourselves time to consider most carefully what both have said before continuing this debate and finally voting on the ... ah, proposals before us. Meanwhile, I do think we should give some attention also to the demonstration at The Hok. While I take Excellency Stent's point that the place is finally in the very capable hands of the Mobile Operations Unit, and I think we need have no fears concerning their efficiency, we do want to feel sure that we have done our utmost to avoid any situation where it might be necessary to deploy them. Still, we do have sixteen days. So I propose we meet again a week today to answer the proposals put before us if need be, and at any rate to consider very carefully the role of the Bureau of Advice and Investigation in the particular context of the demonstration at The Hok. Am I seconded?'

Argand, in a cold sweat, was about to lift an arm weighted with lead, when to his surprise and relief he saw that Commissioner Stent was there ahead of him.

'Then we vote.'

Gapp and Wynand against. The rest for. Motion carried. Meeting closed.

As they milled around at the door preparing to leave, Prinz took Gapp's hand and said, 'Helmut, you are so right about most things, as always. What it all comes down to, does it not, is that the real danger is *people*?' Then he put a paw on Argand's shoulder. 'Jan, an Englishman I much admire once said that in politics a week is a long time. Let's see what happens between now and then, shall we?'

Argand detested politics – but he was grateful that he had a week to think out whether or not it was his duty to defend his bureau or merely the poor functionaries who did their best to serve it.

8

Argand lacked resources. Where most men in his domestic situation, or, more accurately, deprived of domesticity, seek recreation in mild dissipation, and a few in the arts, Argand rejected both. To over-eat every night and get tipsy would have been to surrender to the beast, the animal side of our nature which his upbringing had taught him to abhor. And the arts were, for him, for the most part a confidence trick. He enjoyed, indeed idiosyncratically appreciated, the seventeenth-century painting of the Province and its neighbours. He rather thought he liked Mozart but had found that almost invariably concerts included other composers as well. And the only good thing about fiction was that it honestly proclaimed itself as such – and what sensible man will waste his time with something that is made up?

Consequently it was to his office that he returned after this meeting and, while the summer twilight gathered glaucously on the pavement above him, and the mewling swifts swooped low down the deserted street, he immersed himself in his files.

In four weeks they had received forty-eight complaints, excluding those relating to guest workers. There were a further thirty-six of these, but Argand had decided they should be treated separately. The Turks and Yugoslavs who did the less well-paid and nastier jobs in Brabt had no citizens' rights at all. It was therefore almost impossible for the bureau to help them.

Of the forty-eight, thirteen had been dropped as soon as one of his investigators called on the complainant; and, of the remaining thirty-five, six had been withdrawn at a later stage. Nineteen out of forty-eight.

Why?

Progress in those left had been slow. Indeed, only three cases had been concluded: two in favour of the complainants, one in favour of the police. In none of them had the examining magistrate felt it necessary to recommend further proceedings in higher courts; the reprimands and short terms of suspension it was in his power to hand out had been thought sufficient. One involved the wife of a gem dealer who had objected to being called a fat Jewess, (all right, I am fat, I am Jewish, but do I need a fat goy in uniform to remind me every time I cross the road?); and the other a dockers' union picket who had been too brusquely hustled when trying to stop a container full of spare tank parts destined for Brazil from entering the dockyard. In both cases the complainants had pull.

Of those pending, the one that gave him most concern was that involving the death of Wilhelm Koonig. The ferocity with which the case was being conducted by both sides had surprised him and had left Ensign Tremp quite bewildered. And now there had been this emergency meeting of the Committee of Public Safety. Was this, was it all, did it add up to a conspiracy against his fledgeling bureau? With a half-grimace, half-smile he recalled Dr Liszt's advice that a man in his position should not write off such feelings as paranoia: the chances were that they were well grounded.

His door clicked open. He looked up. Dm Madjen stood on the threshold blinking greyly through tinted spectacles.

'Goodness,' he asked, and his tone was quite unusually kind, 'do you often work as late as this?'

She shrugged. 'Office staff are so inefficient these days.

And illiterate too. I like to check everything.'

'You're right, of course. But don't overdo it.'

'No, Excellency. I take care of myself.' She smiled a grim, thin smile. 'You should too.'

His high brows lifted, then he too smiled.

'Did you wish to see me about something?'

She hesitated, seemed to draw on an inner reserve, came a step or two further into the room.

'Perhaps I am being impertinent.'

Argand's eyebrows became more Punch-like than ever.

'And perhaps not.'

'Well. It's not at all to do with the bureau. But I thought you should . . . I thought you might like to see these.'

With a quick, awkward, shy gesture she placed a sheaf of papers on his desk.

He picked them up. Expensively printed leaflets or handouts – at first sight the sort of circulars one connects with an advertising campaign for encyclopedias or a book club.

'What are they?' He glanced at the mast-head of the top sheet, which was in the form of a letter but with the name of the addressee blank. *The Brabanter Movement for Moral Regeneration, Incorporating the Friends of Brabt and the Festival of Moral Regeneration. Patrons: Archbishop Oldbrod, Count Rupert Hohlenstein, Baron de Merlc.*

'Excellency, this *is* impertinent, but . . . but . . .'

She was pink now, lost for words.

'Do please go on, Dm Madjen.'

'I just know you'll agree . . . after working for you for these few weeks, well, I think I know how you . . . anyway, do please read them. Please.'

And to his amazement, she fled.

The letter was 'signed' (irritating pretence) by Christian Merck, head of the ecumenical council of the United

Reformed Church of Brabt. It assumed that its reader felt as wretched as the author at the moral and spiritual decline of Brabanter life and listed various symptoms of the disease: levelling tendencies in education; abortion; the alienation of youth – the subcultures that existed round drugs and rock music; the libertarian 'reforms' passed by a spineless Moot that put political expediency before more lasting values . . . It concluded by saying that the accompanying literature pointed the way to a cleansing of the Augean Stables and appealed to the reader for support, in the first place financial support.

Yes. Dm Madjen *had* been impertinent. But recalling the witness, the vigil for the festival he had seen in Rinusplatz, Argand was not surprised. His own father had been a lay preacher in the Church of Inner Salvation and in his childhood he had often met the sort of deeply committed Christians who will risk giving offence and even being reprimanded for their faith.

There followed a six-panelled foldout on glossy paper with three sections purporting to have been written by the three patrons. There were charismatic photographs of each, and again facsimile signatures rounded them off.

Archbishop Oldbrod had been removed from the Catholic Primacy and threatened with excommunication for refusing to give up the Tridentine Mass and accept other Vatican II resolutions; he had already lost the support of the lower levels of the Brabanter Hierarchy, who are notoriously radicalised. He now called for a return to the old values, for a resurgence of Brabanter pride and independence, a concerted resistance to evil influences from outside, both those of western consumerism and the godless materialism of the east.

Count Rupert, a remote cousin of the Grand Duke and Colonel-in-Chief of the Legion of Veterans, called for a return to the values that two generations of Brabanters had fought for in two world wars. He spoke much of how modern Brabt had betrayed the sacrifice of its fathers, but forbore to mention (and Argand had forgotten) that he had served before Stalingrad with the thousand-strong Brabt Sea Eagle Brigade and that the nucleus of his Legion was composed of the three hundred survivors.

Baron de Merle, Chairman of EUREAC, wrote of the need for a return to the highest standards of loyalty between workers and management, of how agreements should be honoured and breaches of contract punished, of how traditional Brabanter self-discipline would have to be rediscovered if the challenge of the new technologies was to be met, of how there was no substitute for Brabanter craftsmanship on the shop floor, and of how the Province would have to accept that the day of the guest worker was over.

Argand read all this in two minds. On the surface with uncritical acceptance – it was after all the received wisdom of his caste, the ideology not of the ruling class but the one imposed by it from above on all those who most faithfully and willingly serve it. But underneath he felt a nagging dissatisfaction which exposed itself as a sense of irritated boredom. He passed on to the second pamphlet.

This was the work of one Wolfgang Dreiser, a conservative member of the Moot and a man thought to be the intellectual force behind a group of new rightists known as the Club. It was entitled: 'The Friends and their Strategy'. Argand's interest quickened as he read it.

Dreiser argued that the trouble with ordinary, decent, hard-working folk everywhere, but especially in Brabt, was that they were essentially private people who minded their own business and expected others to do likewise. In itself this was, he wrote, a prime virtue, but at times like these, when all the standards such people live for are threatened, it was a weakness – for where others who did band together in unions, or in tightly knit political parties, or even as terrorists, were able to display an apparent but spurious strength, the great majority of people left their very real strength unused, untapped.

The difficulty was that right-minded, independent people did not easily ally themselves to organisations which then demanded their obedience body and soul – and this was surely because they had already made that commitment but to something much higher and nobler than any faction or sect, namely to Brabt, City and Province, Nation and State; and in return they rightly expected the state and its institutions to propagate and protect the standards they lived for.

'It is,' Dreiser wrote, 'an indisputable fact that the state has failed in that duty. And that the good people of Brabt are aware that this has happened is something they should make clear to the state, so the state will be prompted to put its house in order.

'How best to do this? The Vigil of Witness in Rinusplatz and the ensured success of the Festival of Moral Regeneration point the way. What is needed is an alliance, nationwide, of friends, the Friends of Brabt. It will, in the first instance, be a very loose organisation demanding nothing of its members except a small subscription, but through it might be channelled and expressed the hopes and fears, aspirations and beliefs of its members. Then it could organise mass lobbying of the Moot to counter the unions, it could promote peaceful marches and demonstrations, get up petitions and so on. Churches, clubs and so on already in existence will be welcome to affiliate themselves.'

Argand was especially pleased to note the next point. The Friends would not be a political party. There were enough of those already. But Dreiser hoped that through its efforts the conservative parties and the right wing of the PBDC would rediscover their energy, their principles, and through them the PBDC as a whole would be brought back to its real function, its real duty, as the guardian of the state and its institutions; it would disavow its alliance with the Socialist Party, which had fallen into the hands of Trotskyites and worse, and turn away from the weak, woolly, dangerous ways of the last decade or so, from the sloppy so-called liberalisation and reforms its uneasy bedfellow had imposed upon it.

Dreiser concluded by praying – yes, praying – that the culmination of the Festival of Moral Regeneration on Sunday might mark the foundation of the Friends as a national force: he urged all who shared his beliefs to attend and to declare publicly their witness before they left the stadium; the opportunity would be there.

The last sheet listed the organisations that had declared support for the festival and the Friends. There was what looked like an impressive number of industrial companies and a bank or two, but Argand knew they were all subsidiaries of EUREAC: they could all be said to stand for de Merle and little else. Even so, it added up to about fifteen per cent of the industrial and financial power of Brabt, and no doubt others would follow this lead, especially those who owed EUREAC a favour or were hoping to negotiate contracts. Then there were several churches including the Authentic Catholic Church of Brabt – ex-Archbishop Oldbrod's breakaway from Rome – and many of the Protestants, including the Church of Inner Salvation. This impressed Argand. Although he had rejected its fundamentalism, he retained a nostalgic respect for it. He was reluctant to believe its followers would knowingly support anything that did not have the very best of intentions.

Finally, there were seven or eight more diverse groups such as the Society of Protestant School Teachers, the Campaign for Clean Energy (a pro-nuclear-power organisation clandestinely funded by the PBDC), the Venturers (who recruited unemployed youths and trained them in survival and rescue techniques but used them as stewards in demonstrations against guest labour), a body called the Chevaliers of Christ the Purifier and another called the Handmaids of the Lord of which Argand knew nothing.

He sat for a while in his silent office and brooded. He had after all been stirred, no doubt of it. There was much he approved in a routine way but also there was an excitement, an anger that appealed, something that touched a suppressed nerve that wanted to be vindictive, have its revenge, take it out on *them*, on those who spoil things.

At last, but feeling darkly guilty as he did so, he pulled out his cheque book. 10,000 gelds, he wrote. Then altered the first nought to a five. 15,000.

And Petra Madjen? Impertinent, yes. But he was glad she had had the courage to do what she had done.

9

'But you are a Chevalier of Christ the Purifier.'

'Yes, Counsellor.'

'And proud of it, no doubt.'

'Certainly, Counsellor.'

'The Counsellor for the Bureau of Advice and Investigation has already described the Chevaliers as a neo-fascist organisation. What is your response to that?'

The young man, lean, dark-haired, sallow-skinned, with pock-marked face, dressed scrupulously in the well-pressed and spotless parade uniform of a State Security Trooper, hesitated for a moment. Then he half shrugged, and jerked his head upwards.

'Counsellor, I don't understand the question.'

A rustle of papers, a movement of heads, a susurration of tiny whispers.

'Let me rephrase.' Counsellor appearing for the State Security Police hitched up his purple gown. 'What do the Chevaliers of Christ the Purifier stand for?'

The young man relaxed, almost smiled.

'For the moral regeneration of Brabt,' he said.

'No more questions.'

The counsellor appearing for the Bureau of Advice and Investigation was on his feet.

'Were you acting for the moral regeneration of Brabt when you hit Wilhelm Koonig with your illegal blackjack?'

'Objection,' cried the first counsellor. 'Witness has already stated that he tapped the deceased with his standard police truncheon to encourage him to answer questions. And that he did so in pursuance of the instructions already given him.'

'Objection upheld.'

His Serenity Examining Magistrate Vustouk was an old man run physically to seed, fat, with rheumy eyes, one of which was blind and left grotesquely uncovered; but he retained his native wit, to which was married an unerring belief in the right of every case to be judged on its own merits. He flicked over a page of the ledger in front of him and glanced above his eyeglass at the counsellors. 'Any more questions?'

They shook their heads.

'State Security Trooper Kral may stand down. The court adjourns until tomorrow, when I will hear speeches, which need not be long, in summation.'

He stood, all stood with him, and the Chief Clerk intoned a minuscule prayer in praise of justice and the Grand Duke.

Earlier, during the midday recess, Tremp had sat with Argand in the small room that had been allotted to him during the course of the inquiry. During the week Tremp had lost some of his neat dapper look and his clothes (a formal suit now, but cut stylishly) were uncharacteristically dishevelled. He explained again what he had already outlined in his daily reports, how he and the bureau's counsellor had gone into the inquiry solely with the aim of establishing that the State Security Police and Trooper Kral had broken the law: that was the point at issue, and all other considerations were irrelevant.

Things had seemed to go well for the first two days.

Several important facts had been proved, apparently unassailably: that Kral had hit Koonig with a short length of hosepipe filled with lead shot; that the blow could have caused the hairline fracture in the skull and the brain haemorrhage from which Koonig died. Counsellor had been at pains to point out that Koonig's death was, at this stage, only material in so far as it indicated the force with which the illegal blow had been delivered. It was not his concern to pre-empt His Serenity's prerogative of deciding whether or not more serious charges should later be laid against Kral.

Casualty doctor, radiologist, brain surgeon all supported this evidence, though chinks had begun to appear when the surgeon under cross-examination asserted that, had Koonig been treated within twelve hours, he would probably have survived. He also refused to assert definitely that the blow had been caused by the blackjack – simply he confirmed that there was nothing about the injury to indicate that it could not have been caused by the weapon in question. Yes, a fall downstairs could have had the same result, though would have caused other contusions as well; a blow with a bottle might have had the same effect.

Counsellor concluded his case by showing that a blackjack and insignia of the Chevaliers of Christ the Purifier had been found in Trooper Kral's locker at the State Security head-quarters. Without calling Kral, he had established that the blackjack was quite definitely an illegal weapon, even in the hands of a policeman, and that the Chevaliers were a semi-secret group of men dedicated to the harassment of all social deviants whose activities were not sufficiently (according to its members) restricted by the law. These were shown to include homosexuals, pot-smokers, unemployed guest workers claiming social benefits, people who opposed the government's defence and energy policies, men and women who walked about in the open air with no clothes on, and people with long and unkempt hair. Counsellor had concluded that, since almost all these categories were present in the person of Wilhelm Koonig, it was highly probable that

Chevalier Kral had been tempted to exert more than usual force when he struck a blow that would have been illegal even if lightly given. Finally, Margarethe and others from the commune testified that they had all been handled roughly, illegally detained, and that property had been taken and returned only many days later or not at all. And they were all sure that the weapon used on Koonig was Exhibit 'A', the blackjack.

Counsellor for the Bureau of Advice and Investigation had not called Licentiate Petersen, and Licentiate Petersen was very angry since it was he who had laid the official complaint.

'Well,' said Tremp, 'Counsellor Botha's turn came to call witnesses on behalf of Kral and the State Security Police and he's taken the whole thing apart. The State Security Deputy here in Brichtzee gave evidence that at least five members of the commune were on file as dangerous, and that there was evidence that pointed to a conspiracy to sabotage The Hok plant. He had raided the hotel without asking for a warrant because he felt that under the circumstances it was important that no warning should be given. Our man came back rather well on that, by pointing out that the two previous raids by the Rural Guard were surely warning enough and he challenged the Deputy with malicious harassment. Well, what he said looks good on paper, but it didn't come across that convincingly in court . . .' Tremp passed a tired hand over his eyes, then felt in his pocket for a handkerchief and blew his nose. 'Especially when the Deputy added that a map of The Hok had been found amongst Koonig's possessions.'

Argand was conscious that Tremp was in a poor way. The young man was torn almost schizophrenically apart by the job he had been landed in: a moral division exacerbated by the fact that he was keen, hard-working, clever, ambitious and young and so suffered from a very human (as Argand saw

57

it) desire to win. However distasteful he found it to bring a case against his colleagues in State Security, it was still a fight, and he did not want to lose it.

Tremp continued his resumé. Next, Counsellor Botha established that most of the commune were members of the League of Marxist–Leninist Militants, a group dedicated to the overthrow of society as we know it. Then, using evidence supplied by neighbours, he built up a picture of the commune carefully calculated to upset the sensibilities of any decent, ordinary, hard-working Brabanter. He topped off the edifice by re-calling Margarethe first, then calling two other witnesses who had not appeared before.

Margarethe admitted tearfully that she had been Koonig's mistress (though she preferred the term 'love-friend') and that both of them were drawing social security benefits; that she had found that cannabis soothed his headaches and that she had given him plenty in spite of Petersen's interdiction on the stuff; that there were bottles in the room where Koonig was ill – but no alcohol, she insisted, only Pepsi, Fanta and mineral water. Then Botha produced a riot-stick – a short thin black thing, strong but not heavy – and hesitatingly she agreed it did not look unlike Exhibit 'A', the blackjack, but added that it was rigid. Botha held the riot-stick between thumb and forefinger, exactly in the centre, and rocked it up and down. Margarethe agreed that this produced an optical illusion of flexibility.

The bureau's counsellor re-examined and she reasserted that on the whole she thought Kral had hit Koonig with the blackjack.

The next witness Botha called was Eric Lanning, an out-of-work joiner. He was fat, pasty-faced, had lank brown hair and wore spectacles. Although not a living-in member of the commune, he agreed that he was sympathetic to the League of Marxist–Leninist Militants and that he had spent quite a lot of time in the Hotel Bristol. He asserted that, the day before the State Security raid, Koonig, while under the influence of cannabis, had accepted a dare that he could break an empty litre bottle of Pepsi on his head without unduly hurting himself. He had hit himself twice, without breaking the bottle, and then given up.

The last witness was described as Hans Braun, student. He was tall, thin, fit, with a half-established blond beard and manic blue eyes. He simply asserted that Koonig had fallen downstairs two days before the raid.

Here Argand had interrupted Tremp's account. 'Were they "V-men"?' He used the term current in Brabt, as it is in West Germany, for *agents provocateurs*, infiltrators.

Tremp pursed his lips. 'I don't know.'

'And only Commissioner General Gapp can tell us. And he can refuse to answer or insist we make no use of the information if it turns out that they are.'

Finally, Botha had called Kral, and that part of the hearing Argand had seen for himself. He had not been convinced by the State Trooper – there had been a pertness about the way he gave his evidence that argued both thorough rehearsal and a contempt for the proceedings. The blackjack was a souvenir, he had said, and it had never left his locker since he put it there three years ago. At the Hotel Bristol he had used his riot-stick when Koonig refused to say whether or not the cardboard box in which the map of The Hok plant had been found belonged to him.

At that point, His Serenity had made one of his rare interruptions. Again looking over his eyeglass, he had said in the throaty voice which occasionally fluked into an old man's treble, 'Let me be quite clear, young man. You are not denying that you hit Koonig with a weapon.'

'But not with my blackjack, Serenity.'

Vustouk sighed. There was a long pause while apparently

he thought of rephrasing his question. Then he merely said, 'Be direct with me, young man.'

At last Kral blushed, then paled. Another silence ensued, during which he clearly struggled to remember what he had been asked.

'Serenity, I *tapped* Koonig with my riot-stick when he refused to indicate whether or not the map was his. That is all.'

Serenely, with his old-fashioned glass-nibbed fountain pen, Vustouk had made another note in his ledger.

10

Outside the courtroom, in the wide, marble-floored corridor, seven or eight reporters were gathered. As the spectators, witnesses and so on, flooded out, Argand was surprised that it was he they were after. Brought up sharp by a flash going off in his face, he blinked, twisted his head back and forth, and momentarily planted a hand on Tremp's forearm, almost as if he were seeking reassurance.

'Excellency, how have the proceedings gone? Are you satisfied with the way your case has been put?'

'I am entirely satisfied with the very professional conduct of our counsellor.'

'Do you think your new bureau will win this case?'

'It would be most improper for me to anticipate His Serenity's judgement.'

'Excellency, is it true that there is bad feeling between you and Commissioner Gapp of State Security?'

This was clearly the key question, the one the reporters had come to ask. Sure that he now knew what was happening, Argand squared his shoulders and faced the reporter who had asked the question.

'There is absolutely no truth in that. Relations between me and the Excellent Commissioner have never been more cordial.'

'How can that be when your bureau challenges his force's activities at every step?'

'It is not true that my bureau does anything of the sort. We pursue inquiries only when we think it probable that the law has been broken.'

Someone at the back of the group let out a bray of sarcastic laughter – its meaning was clear: for him at least everything the State Security Police did was illegal.

'Is it true that, at a recent meeting of the Public Safety Committee, Commissioner Gapp attempted to have your bureau closed down?'

'You cannot possibly expect me to comment in any way at all on the proceedings of a state committee. Now, gentlemen, I am busy even if you are not. That is enough.' He turned to Tremp. 'I'm going to my car – it's in the private carpark behind the building. Try to find out what lies behind all this and tell me there.'

'Is it true that there is bad blood between you and Gapp? That he was responsible for an official complaint laid against you two years ago, and a consequent official reprimand?'

Argand felt anger swell. He pushed bear-like through the tiny crowd, allowing his elbow to collide heavily with a camera on his way. I hope I've damaged it, he thought.

Ten minutes later Tremp found him in his official car, seated behind his driver. As the electronically operated window whirred down, he handed in a folded newspaper.

'I think this is it, Chief.'

Argand nodded. He did not need to unfold it. He recognised readily enough the format of *Slik Stien*, a satirical paper named after a Brabanter folk hero cognate with the German Till. As Commissioner for Public Order he had tried to have it closed, although in fact it had once praised him for being the only Honest Commissioner in Brabt, perhaps the only honest policeman. Before his large black Peugeot had left the centre of Brichtzee, he had read the brief paragraph on the front page set below a montage of photos of him and Gapp, back to back and apparently muttering obscenities at each other. It said no more than had been implied in the reporters' questions: that there was ancient bad feeling between them, that Gapp had used the Committee of Public Safety in an attempt to have the new bureau closed down.

Argand did not bother with the rest of the paper, which he found invariably distasteful or worse. But he speculated for a long time on the source of the leak. In the end he decided it could only be Gapp himself. And that worried him. He did not like Gapp. He knew that Gapp did not like him. But until now he had never had reason to doubt the ex-soldier's professionalism.

11

What of note occurred during the next ten days – that is, up to the rally at The Hok – can be put briefly enough.

On Thursday His Serenity Examining Magistrate Vustouk delivered judgement. In it, the old man, half-blind as he was, made it clear that he despised cleverness and learning. Counsellors and witnesses had displayed far too much cleverness and learning and had consequently wasted public money and public time spinning out over six working days a matter that could have been settled in a morning.

The points at issue were whether or not the State Security Police had observed the proper formalities before raiding the Hotel Bristol, and whether or not Trooper Kral had struck Koonig illegally. Blackjack or riot-stick was immaterial – what was material was whether or not Koonig had been attempting to escape, or offering violence to Kral, or anyone else in the room, at the time.

Much flummery had been heaped round these simple, straightforward points, but simple and straightforward they remained. No one had even tried to pretend that the raid had been legalised by a warrant – therefore the Deputy of State Security who had ordered it was in error. He was hereby reprimanded and would lose six months' seniority. As for Kral, no attempt had been made either to deny he struck the blow or justify it according to law. He too would receive a second-degree reprimand. However, Vustouk felt he must go further. Evidence had been brought, probably irrelevantly,

64

that Koonig had died as a result of the blow and, albeit this evidence had been contested, equally irrelevantly, His Serenity believed he was now justified in handing on a full transcript of the inquiry to the Director of State Prosecution. It would be for him to decide whether or not Kral should be charged with criminal manslaughter. Pending the Director's decision, Kral was to be suspended with pay, and was also ordered to report once a day to the Brichtzee Rural Guard, who would of course be responsible for his arrest if further charges were to be brought.

On Saturday Argand watched TV: the special coverage on Channel Three of the Festival of Moral Regeneration at Brabt City Stade. His feelings towards the whole business had soured a little – State Trooper Kral was undoubtedly an unpleasant customer and his membership of the Chevaliers of Christ the Purifier did them no credit – and what he saw confirmed this change of heart. In the first place it was something of a flop. There were indeed fifteen thousand people there, but nearly eleven thousand had arrived under the auspices of one organisation or another; of the general, uncommitted public there were fewer than five thousand. Christian Merck declared it a most promising start; Count Rupert praised the high turnout and smartness of the Veterans; Wolfgang Dreiser, member of the Moot and political theoriser, was not available for comment.

There were processions, bands, hymn-singing, speeches and sermons. At the end of it all, the various organisations paraded rather untidily round the perimeter of the stadium carrying torches which smoked excessively and dropped burning tar on the grass. Amongst them were forty men or youths who wore hoods. These were the Chevaliers and they wore the hoods out of modesty; the glory of their service should, a spokesman had said, reflect only Christ's glory;

none wished to gain personal kudos through being known as a member.

No figure was given as to how many had declared themselves ready to join the Friends of Brabt. Next day *The Brabanter* estimated that eight hundred had done so.

On Tuesday the Committee of Public Safety met again to consider Excellent Commissioner Wynand's proposals. Excellent Commissioner Jan Argand spoke forcefully for almost ten minutes in defence of his bureau. During the four weeks it had been fully functional, one thing had become apparent to him: that it was now common police practice to ignore the law and standing orders; in several cases he felt sympathy, but the practice was nevertheless to be utterly condemned and stamped out. If the law and standing orders needed to be changed, then that was a matter for the Moot. Meanwhile, he felt most strongly that his bureau was performing an essential function in bringing back to ordinary policemen a proper sense of their responsibilities and the very proper limitations imposed upon them. He kept his eyes well away from Gapp as he said this.

He made no mention of his growing certainty that complainants were being systematically intimidated, nor his suspicion that there was somewhere in the background a centralised, organised force at work against him. He had already been hospitalised once by his enemies as a schizoparanoid.

Gapp reiterated his fears that neither he, nor Public Order, nor the Rural Guard would be able to do their jobs properly at The Hok with the new bureau on their backs and he now had even clearer indications that an attempt would be made to sabotage the plant, indications which might have been proof had not his men been subjected to the inquiry at Brichtzee. Prinz sucked thoughtfully on his pipe for a time and then proposed that Argand and his team of eight operatives should be at The Hok as observers. They would then have first-hand experience of the event, would be able to judge for themselves if situations had arisen where complaints against the police might be justified. He also suggested that they should not act on complaints until the whole affair was safely over.

They voted on Wynand's proposals. Gapp and Wynand for; Argand, Traffic Control and Stent for Crime against. Prinz and Pranck of Public Order abstained.

On the way out, Prinz smiled beatifically at Argand, put his paw on the Commissioner's shoulder.

'You did well, Jan, very well. Almost too well. Almost over the top, eh? And no real need, you know. Traffic Control and Crime were always on your side, and so was my deciding vote if need be.'

That the voting had been fixed in advance left Argand dispirited. Not for the first time in his career, he felt he was being manipulated.

PART TWO: DEMONSTRATION

12

The River Flot meanders on a roughly south-east to north-west course, leaving about two thirds of the Province to its left – fertile flat lands and then, towards the Belgian and Luxembourg borders, coalfields and heavy industry – and one third to its right: less fertile fens, salt pastures and salt marshes. Its estuary, six kilometres wide at low tide, is dominated by two industrial complexes: to the south, the EUREAC chemical plant and oil refinery, recently enlarged by the Spartshaven Project; on the right, north-eastern bank, a nuclear-power complex, including an experimental reactor, a reprocessing plant, a research station and the sites of three more projected reactors. These are spread over a spit of high land with sandstone crags at its highest points and sand-dunes towards the seashore, while on the river side the site drops to flat salt pastures reclaimed from the tidal river basin a hundred years ago. Because the original spit of sand-stone, before the reclamation took place, was shaped like a long hafted hook, the area is known as The Hok, and the complex as The Hok plant.

From the distance – and only the people who work there see it from anything else – this is dominated by a one-hundred-metre-high chimney; then there are spherical coolers, more chimneys, and finally an untidy sprawl of blank buildings, many of them windowless. Amongst the dunes, seven giant derricks mark the site of the new reactors.

There are two separate approaches. Running more or less

directly from the City of Brabt are a railway and a major road, a spur off the Brabt–Antwerp autoroute. These carry the radioactive materials the site requires or is in business to reprocess, the construction materials and a large part of the workforce. For reasons never publicised, no one who works there seems keen to live near the plant, although apart from the complex itself the surrounding countryside is not unattractive. Grey sheep drift over pastures of coarse grass; nearer the river, flocks of marsh and sea birds wheel against high skies or strut across mudflats. Dramatic cloudscapes project shafts and pools of cool sunlight on grey water, on ochre- and olive-tinted land; and on the tide huge ships glide purposefully by. But as the railway and road approach the plant, houses become sparser, villages derelict, and there are fewer sheep. In spite of government assurances that every carcase is carefully screened, people no longer buy the once highly prized meat.

The second approach is from the north and east through a loose complex of country lanes that wind across gorse-covered heath, through small pinewoods, round outcrops of sandstone. These serve the villages and the one small town, St Romain, on the coast. St Romain was once a popular resort like Brichtzee to the south and also supported an inshore fishing fleet. But, like Brichtzee, it suffered from the migration of holidaymakers to the south of Europe. The level of radioactivity found in the local fish, especially in the delicious crabs, is five times as high as that found a hundred kilometres away; and fishermen find that the markets will not touch perch and lampreys covered with wart-like spots. In fifteen years the population has dropped by twenty per cent.

As the spit of sandstone narrows, the network of country roads contracts until only two are left. The surfaces of both become broken and uneven, the banks are left uncut, and shrubs lean across the carriageway. Eventually both are abruptly closed by a barrier that runs for eight kilometres from the river, across the reclaimed pastures, up into the sandstone outcrops, across heath, down into the dunes, and so to the sea. It consists of two fences with a deep ditch between: there are watchtowers set at kilometre intervals, and notices announce high-tension electrified wires and patrolling guard dogs. This barrier is broken near the river by the railway and the motorway, and traversed at two other points by power lines strung from giant pylons. These march across the fens, into the hillier farmland beyond, and thence to Holland and Germany, to the European grid. It all appears, and is intended to be, impregnable to anything but a full-scale military assault.

Through these country lanes and finally up the last two roads to the perimeter itself came, in the last week of August, the advance guard of an army, though not a military one. 2CVs, Renault 4s, Daf pickups, VW trucks and campers brought tents, scaffolding for stages, mobile kitchens and mobile latrines, public-address systems, first-aid posts; local traders set up stalls to sell the spicy sausages of the region and radioactive crab. Amongst them, shunned, ignored, at best grudgingly obeyed, moved Traffic Police, Public Order Police and the Rural Guard, each in their distinctive uniforms and, more discreetly though no less numerous, State Security Troopers, most of whom were in plain clothes. Paratroopers in the green uniform of the Mobile Operations Unit watched from the towers, and occasionally a track-mounted armoured rocket launcher could be seen trundling through the dunes behind the fence. Command posts were set up at the points where the roads met the fence and here were deployed armoured Panhard and Saviem personnel carriers, water cannon, and Hotspur Land Rovers equipped with CS gas dischargers. By Thursday evening the population along the fence had risen from nil to an estimated four thousand. Late on Friday morning the first of the demonstrators proper appeared, and at the same time heavy low clouds began to build up in the south-west, their purplish blackness providing a dramatic backcloth for the high stacks of the EUREAC plant across the estuary and then for the giant chimney and white cooling spheres of the nuclear site itself.

For a time the whole scene was lit by fitful gleams of yellow light, but as the sun moved west and sank, the darkness thickened unnaturally early. The demonstrators came on – in cars for the most part small, old and shabby or wildly decorated, but some large with caravans; in modern shiny coaches laced with chrome, on motorbikes and mopeds, on bicycles and on foot – at least on foot from the nearest railway station ten kilometres away. Although many shared a sort of uniform – long hair, denims, anoraks, deeply cleated walking boots – there were many, far too many, Commissioner Argand thought, who were, well, ordinary. There were working people *en famille*, and he questioned their sense of responsibility in bringing babes in arms to such a place; there were people middle-aged or older whose smooth faces and good-quality town clothes indicated teachers, engineers, technicians. There was even a group of nuns.

By six o'clock the flow had begun to ease off, yet, spread out over the heath, parked and camping in the tiny fields carved out from the encroaching gorse, sheltered behind outcrops of sandstone or huddled in the dunes near the sea, there were already an estimated twenty-two thousand, some sixteen thousand of whom turned up at the perimeter fence to hear the first of the promised rock concerts. As the group, Kreep from Amsterdam, took the stage, the first heavy drops

74

fell. Forty minutes later, with the rain now steady and heavy, they gave up, and through the gloom the audience trudged and splashed its way back to tents, caravans and campers.

The rain continued throughout the night and by mid-morning on the Saturday – the chief day of the rally, the day set for the major speeches – had created problems. Almost as many people now wanted to leave as were still arriving, and the whole network of tiny lanes was jammed solid. Vehicles that tried to escape or get in by cutting across country stuck, wheels spinning, in wet sand; hitch-hikers apologetically dismounted and cheerily trudged past the columns of stationary cars, vans and coaches, but then cursed the swathes of muddy water scythed over them by slithering mopeds. The latrines flooded, the kitchens closed, and the Brabanter meteorological office announced no change in the weather for twenty-four hours.

After a very near miss in low cloud, the officer in charge of Traffic Police helicopters ordered them grounded: thus Commissioner Wynand of the Rural Guard was stranded in his headquarters behind the St Romain town hall and had to play his part by radio in the meeting called at the more southerly of the two command posts – present were the other Commissioners, representatives of the organisers, and a major from the Mobile Operations Unit.

The meeting, held in a Saviem S95 command vehicle, seemed as certain as the traffic outside to congeal into messy deadlock. The organisers said that it was too late to cancel completely, though they were prepared to abandon Sunday's programme; on the other hand, the police declared that the hazards to life and property were increasing with every centimetre of rain that fell. Yet within each camp there were gradations of response to the appalling weather. For once Wynand, his voice squawking over the radio, was at odds with Gapp. He wanted to close the Dutch border, halt the chartered trains that were still due to arrive and deploy a cordon of troops and police ten kilometres from the perimeter that would let demonstrators out but not in. Gapp's view, however, was that the damage to local property would be a charge on the organisers, that the whole wretched affair would be a serious setback to the anti-nuclear movement – in short, having taken the rope they should be allowed to hang themselves.

Pranck, Public Order, was outraged. Responsibility for the integrity of the perimeter was shared between him and Gapp, and, as visibility dropped and the number of demonstrators near it increased, he doubted if he had the resources available to maintain it without resorting to maximum measures. He went on to argue that deprived of music and speeches the temper of the crowd would become increasingly volatile – a point one of the organisers, a schoolteacher, took up. Under normal circumstances he was confident his stewards would be able to contain the tiny minority of irresponsible extremists, anarchists and the like, but now he would like to see the area actually open to the demonstrators restricted, with help from the police, to a more manageable size.

The major from the Mobile Operations Unit made his one contribution at this point. He was a tall, lean figure in olive green, red beret and MOBOP badge – a winged dagger above a scroll and their motto 'Greater Love Hath No Man'. He had arrived from the plant with three paratroopers armed with Beretta sub-machine-guns and a rocket launcher, and he had watched the civilian police with a sullen incredulity.

'I shouldn't concentrate the crowd,' he said. 'If you do, then when the perimeter goes you will maximise the casualty rate. Standing orders are that an area one hundred metres in radius from a breach is to be taken out with saturation mortar and rocket fire. *Then*, we assess the situation.'

The rain rattled like a snare drum on the roof, and the windows of the Saviem were misted up. To Argand's now often slightly disoriented vision, the ill-assorted faces of organisers, police and this murderous young army officer took on a nightmarish quality, an effect enhanced by the flickering, sub-aqueous light cast by the console of CCTV monitors banked at the back of the vehicle.

A radio receiver bleeped, not the one Wynand still occasionally squawked over. Its operator scribbled on a pad and brought the message to Pranck, who changed his glasses to read it, and then changed them back before making his announcement.

'This,' he said, 'is a message from the Sub-Prefect of St Romain. As you know, the mayor is a socialist and Walter Beck is staying with him. He has now proposed that the fish market be opened and the market square outside, and the whole space made available for the rally. Beck will use it for the speech he was going to make here.' He now looked almost despairingly at Argand, who for six years had held the position he was now in and whose admiring subordinate he had been. 'Is this what we should do? Can it be done? That's what we must decide. Can it be done?'

All but Gapp agreed it should be done. No one seemed ready to coordinate the massive redeployment of what now looked like being a rally of one hundred and fifty thousand and the six thousand police, paramilitary and military who were in the area to control them. Pranck and Wynand bickered over the radio, Traffic Control continued to insist that his helicopters must stay grounded. But Gapp reiterated, 'Leave them here and let them stew. They won't get through the fence, they'll just get wet, and eventually they'll go away.' He was smoking through a small holder; letting ash drop on the corner of a map, he turned to the blanked-out windscreen of the Saviem. 'And if, with the weather on their side they do get through, then, as the major has told us, MOBOP have the facilities to deal with them.'

Argand presumed that Gapp was referring to the cadres of the more radically disaffected who, according to his intelligence, were planning an attack. But 'dealing with them' would involve plain, straightforward slaughter. He shook his head to clear the dull ache promoted by the claustrophobic space whose every molecule thudded to the racket of the diesel engine, now functioning as a generator. And Gapp was by no means the only smoker. He pulled maps towards him, squeezed Pranck out of his way. 'Come now,' he said. 'This won't do. They'll soon know out there that Beck intends to speak at St Romain, not here. We've no choice. Just let's make sure it's done properly.'

13

Paul and Mik were by no means anti-nuke freaks – indeed, having been brought up in and escaped from the coalmining area of the Zar, they tended to believe that any source of energy which meant less coalmining had to be good. However, they were drawn by the fringe activities, the dressing-up, the anti-authoritarian side of it, and particularly by some of the more bizarre rock groups attached to it. One of these – Gay Stride – they particularly liked and, according to the rally programme, they would be able to leave the City at nine thirty by train, hear Gay Stride's set outside The Hok plant at about one o'clock and be back at the Aureole by six. Their patron, feeling he owed them something since they had after all so readily dropped their complaint against the police, said he'd arrange cover for them until then.

They should, of course, have known better than to expect a programme of this sort to be anything more than a come-on to persuade waverers that the rally did have side attractions as well as serious purpose. That at any rate was what they were told by a Dutchman in a VW camper who gave them a lift from St Romain railway station towards The Hok. Soon the VW was jammed in a long line of similar vehicles snaking between high banks of sand and sandstone. The road was already a centimetre or more deep in gritty red mud, the rain slipped in a continuous sheet off the windscreen, and the two small boys who shared the back of the VW with Paul and Mik began to whine and grumble. Apparently they were missing a British programme for children which they always watched on Saturday mornings.

It became obvious that there were as many vehicles on the road coming away from The Hok as going towards it and many more pedestrians trudging precariously on the narrow, slimy verge. At last the Dutchman, a lecturer at a teacher training college, wound down his window and tried to find out what was going on. The first two people he asked did not know – they were simply going where stewards and traffic police had directed them. At this point the Dutchman's wife revealed what was apparently a recurring fantasy of hers – that some day the authorities would use one of the mass anti-nuclear demonstrations to stamp out the movement once and for all. Every car, bus, van going to a remote place such as The Hok could be directed by the police into some convenient spot such as a disused quarry and there be bombed or gassed into annihilation. If it were properly organised, she said, it could be months before anyone pieced together what had really happened; the rest of the population would be frightened by the rumours of a massacre, and anyway many would accept it as a good thing. There were, she said, precedents . . .

A steward with an armband – the anti-nuclear device set in a white circle – stuck his dripping head through the window. Briskly, for the hundredth time at least, he explained that the rally had been re-sited in St Romain marketplace, that they were to proceed for a half-kilometre towards The Hok, just as far as a disused sandpit, where traffic police would direct them into the traffic flow back to the town. They were not to attempt a U-turn until they got to the sandpit.

'I told you so,' said the Dutchman's wife, and the eldest of her boys, old enough to understand most of what she had been saying, began to cry in real earnest.

The Dutchman lost his temper, cursed his wife, children,

the human condition and his VW, which had stalled. Paul suggested that he and Mik would get back to St Romain more quickly if they got out and walked. Outside, the steward was brusque with them – he had no idea when or if there was going to be a concert, had never heard of Gay Stride; the main speeches were scheduled for two o'clock and the rally was to be declared closed at seven.

Paul and Mik joined the long line of pedestrians going the other way; in their neat leather coats, close-fitting trousers and smart shoes they stood out from the rest – but rain and mud soon rendered them indistinguishable.

Detective Ensigns Tremp and Focking were installed on a high balcony of the town hall, from where they were able to monitor the flow of traffic and people, reporting back to Argand in the Saviem command vehicle. They were amused, in their very different ways, though not surprised that they were no longer there merely as observers of their colleagues but had been found more useful work. Argand's reputation for crowd control went far beyond the borders of Brabt, and neither of them had much respect for Pranck or Wynand.

Across the road that ran immediately in front of the small town hall was a large piazza, capable, it was reckoned, of holding thirty thousand people. It was lined with small plane trees still hung with fairy lights – on Tremp's suggestion, the bulbs from these were now being unscrewed and removed. At the near end of this space was a small granite dais with three large flagpoles and a war memorial that not only commemorated the dead of Brabt but also the date, in December 1944, of its liberation by British and Canadians. Hence the Brabanter tricolour, its centre panel filled with the arms of the Grand Dukes, was flanked by the Union Jack and the Maple Leaf – all, at that moment, hanging sodden in the rain.

The fish market, a grey, hangar-like building, stood at the far end. Once it had catered for a thriving wholesale trade but now housed only four or five retail stalls. It was an airy, open place; the walls were arched down the sides and entirely open at the end that faced the piazza. Beyond it was the quay and the small artificial harbour with twin moles and a lighthouse.

Focking watched the flow of traffic as it wound through the main thoroughfares and out down on to the promenade that ran on from the harbour. It was in this area that the demonstrators were being asked to park their cars before walking back to the marketplace.

'*Nein danke*,' he said, reading in turn from the yellow badges with red smiling suns that decorated the backs of almost every car. '*Non merci, no thanks, no grazie. Nan danket. Nan trugarez* – where the hell is that?'

'Brittany,' said Tremp. He was scanning the growing crowd in the marketplace and fish market beyond, trying to estimate the numbers so far.

'What about this? *Ez eskerrik asko*.'

'Basque.'

'How the hell do you know that?'

'We did a basic course when the chiefs thought ETA was developing links with Red Spectre.'

Focking grunted, put down his binoculars and took a large mouthful from the sausage sandwich he had left on the balustrade. 'I wish,' he mumbled, 'I'd brought up a beer.'

'Christ!'

'What?'

'You know that State Security Trooper I had to investigate at Brichtzee?'

'The one who knocked a long-haired bastard on the head with a blackjack who then snuffed it?'

'That's the one. Kral. Well, he's down there.'

'Why not? On V-man duty, I expect.'

82

'He shouldn't be. He's suspended. He may end up on a manslaughter charge, so he should be keeping his nose clean.'

'Here's one you won't know. I'll spell it out. D-i-m. D-i-o-l-c-h.'

Tremp laughed. 'No, that's beyond me. But I sure as hell know what it means. You know, I reckon there's a good seven thousand down there already. And another thing. The rain is easing off.'

Focking gave his huge belly laugh, showering crumbs and sausage out into the pigeon-haunted void. 'Fine. Fine. So we turn them all round and send them back to The Hok.' He choked, and through the coughs gasped. 'Jesus . . . Christ . . . I . . . wish . . . I . . . had . . . a . . . beer.'

Mik was bewildered by the presence of such a vast crowd; Paul was quite excited by it all. Round the perimeter of the fish market, stalls had been improvised from the planks and trestles stacked by the normal users, and posters, badges, stationery, pamphlets, even toys like inflatable whales and kites that looked like kites were on sale. Paul sampled cheese from Larzac, village threatened by military installation, south of France; bread from Wyhl in south Germany, agricultural land to be used for a nuclear power station; buckwheat pancakes from Plogoff in Brittany, ditto; sausage from Frankfurt – the runway . . . and pronounced them all good.

'You know, Mik,' he said, 'we could make a feature of crêpes at the Aureole, they'd go well.'

At the furthest end from the town hall a much larger scaffolding was being erected and a panoply of speakers, amplifiers and so on was being wired up. Over the general clamour these occasionally whistled and boomed and once a giant coughed so the sparrows flew out of the high girders in a spinning cat's cradle and wheeled down into the plane trees. 'Eight, nine, ten, just testing.'

'Perhaps we'll hear Gay Stride after all.'

'We won't have time,' said Paul, his mouth full of fruit cake that was called 'Dundee' though it came from somewhere called the Greenham Common Peace Village. 'Not if they don't come on before the speeches. You know, it's stopped raining and I think we ought to be outside and nearer the back. We don't want to be blocked off from the railway station. And perhaps we can find a beer.'

As they made their way through the piazza, the clatter of a helicopter pushed its way up through and eventually over the din of the crowd. It was a big one and it came low across the steep gabled roofs of the old town, seemed almost to brush the steeple of St Romain cathedral, then hovered over the town hall itself.

'Sikorski,' said Paul.

'How do you know that? You're making it up.'

'No. I did a model one from a kit once, when I was a kid. Perhaps it's Walter Beck coming. They said he would.'

The monster slowly descended, finally disappeared behind the clock tower.

'What's that for?' someone nearby asked.

'MOBOP,' another voice replied. 'They always use them. Gunships. Mow us all down. B-b-b-b-b-bang.'

The truth was less sinister. With the perimeter of The Hok almost clear of demonstrators and the cloud ceiling three or four hundred feet higher, Traffic Control had agreed to airlift his colleagues from their Saviem control vehicle to the Rural Guard headquarters just behind the town hall.

Half an hour later Argand rebriefed the six men he had with him. Now that the pattern of movement of both demonstrators and forces of law and order had been established, indeed

84

was not far off complete, he had left it in the hands of Wynand and Pranck. Meanwhile, the changed situation demanded that his own forces should be redeployed. A largish room equipped for briefing had been made available – it had a screen on which he was able to project a blown-up map of the area.

'Our function from now on is to observe. If there is trouble we have to be on the fringes of it, close enough to see, but we must try to keep out of it. We have to be able to estimate the nature and extent of it objectively and the correctness of our colleagues' response to it, and it will be the purpose of any reports we have to make to reflect whatever happens as accurately as possible. We should not see this role in a negative light – by observing what happens as informed but uninvolved outsiders, we may be able to contribute to our techniques of crowd, affray and riot control, and serve a purpose beyond the limited and distasteful one immediately before us.

'We believe a small number of anarchists on one side and a cell of the League of Marxist–Leninist Militants on the other will try to provoke a police response that will appear unacceptable to the liberal and left-wing press, even one that will look savage on television. Gapp's men have located the main anarchist group inside the fish market and to the left of the dais. I think it's reasonable to suppose that they will remain quiet until Walter Beck begins to speak. The situation is made more sensitive by Beck's status as a Minister of State. We cannot allow him to be silenced by a small, unimportant group of louts. But the louts must not be handled too roughly. I think Commissioners Wynand and Pranck have come up with a plan that will serve. You see how the walls of the market are pierced here and here near the dais? These gaps are at present filled with stalls selling badges, pamphlets and so on. The idea is this, and it has been worked out with the closest cooperation of the organisers, who are absolutely with us as far as anarchists and LMLM are concerned. In the run up to Beck's speech, the stalls will be dismantled by their stewards. As soon as the anarchists begin their interruption, the removal of the stalls will be completed, creating a vent through which the Rural Guard will be able to push anyone making a disturbance. Once outside, and out of range of the TV cameras, they will be invited to disperse. If they don't, Public Order officers will move in and make arrests. Now that is the point where stories of police brutality will originate, and I want Brok and Teleman there to see exactly what does happen.'

He took a drink of water, passed the palm of his large hand down one side of his face and across his mouth, then adjusted the projected map so the scale diminished and a wider area round the piazza came within the borders of the screen.

'The LMLM are the other problem, according to Gapp's sources. Brian Tremp here has already come across these particular villains at the Hotel Bristol. According to Gapp, there was a cell operating within the commune there – only three or four but hard cases compared with the rest – so, Brian, you will keep a good lookout for familiar faces. Gapp is convinced that they were planning to breach the perimeter fence at The Hok during Beck's speech – that option has now been closed to them, thanks to the weather, but we may be sure they are planning something. These people are very different from the anarchists, and Gapp links them to Red Spectre. They are closely knit, well organised, disciplined, and they hate Beck. It's not my province to understand all the alliances and feuds of the left, but that's what we've been told.'

Argand looked away from the screen, seemed for a moment to be concentrating on some inner space. To Tremp he seemed older, or perhaps just very tired. Then he gave the slightest of shakes, a shudder almost, and his brown serious eyes re-focused on the small group in front of him.

'That is the problem, you see. Because of the weather, the changed locale of Beck's speech, they are improvising, and Gapp's intelligence sources have yet to catch up with them. But one thing we can be sure of is that they will be doing their utmost to provoke overreaction from the police, and whatever happens they will be claiming afterwards that the police acted brutally and illegally . . . in support of Beck. As I said at the outset, our job is to be objective recorders and assessors of what *really* happens. There are five of us still undeployed. Riggler and I will operate towards the back of the fish market.' His hand swept in a circle over the relevant area on the screen. 'Brecht takes the area in the middle of the piazza, and Tremp and Focking the back; Tremp to the left of the war memorial, Focking to the right. Any questions?'

Tremp raised a hand. 'Apart from the Rural Guards and Public Order details dealing with the anarchists, where are the rest of our people? I mean, if there is trouble, where are the police we are meant to be observing going to come from?'

Again the worried, abstracted expression appeared on Argand's face.

'Basically,' he said, 'from all round. There are foot detachments of Rural Guard and Public Order here, here and here.' He prodded the screen. 'The water cannon and Hotspurs are here and here. And the uniformed branch of State Security Troopers, two hundred of them, are formed up for a baton charge in the quadrangle of the town hall. The plan is, if they have to be used, to open the big doors beneath the council chamber, so they can come out, cross the colonnade, and move down the steps into the square without breaking formation.'

'But that means,' said Tremp, 'there is nowhere for the crowd to go. No vent.'

Argand's serious eyes held his for a moment.

'Precisely,' he said. 'It is not, I need hardly add, an arrangement of my making, nor one that I can approve. Still, Commissioner Gapp is satisfied with it and has returned to Brabt, leaving his men under the command of a squadron commandant. I hope he knows his job.'

14

To be part of a huge crowd in a flat space is to fail to live the experience. One is aware at the most of five or six hundred people around one and, even if one moves through the crowd and causes the five or six hundred slowly to shift and change, they still never add up to more. Hitler knew what he was doing when he used terraced sports stadia for his rallies; the owners of most west European stadia know what they are doing when they refuse permission for their use by left-wing, anti-authoritarian groups.

Catedratika Julia Arendt, Dean-elect of the University Arts Faculty, was also aware of this. She had been attending demonstrations and rallies since she was five years old – that is, for fifty years, though had addressed them only in the last ten. Lifting her arms above her head and her voice into a cry of triumph, yet pitching it carefully to avoid the feedback that had ruined the speech of her predecessor on the dais, she proclaimed, 'Sisters, brothers – I only wish you could stand where I am and see what I can see. Then you would have something to tell your friends at your workplaces on Monday, then indeed you would have something to remember when your grandchildren and great-grandchildren gather around you in the evening of your lives. And, let us be clear, if you *have* grandchildren and great-grandchildren, it will be in no small measure because *you* have chosen to be here today.'

She let her arms drop, seemed to retire into herself, to

reconstitute her energies, and for a moment the magnetism drained away: she became again the small, dark, rather plain and dumpy middle-aged lady she normally appeared to be. But there were cheers and from them she seemed to regain the charge she had expended.

'If, I say, you could only see yourselves, believe in yourselves as a mighty army dedicated to peace and progress, a horde as numerous as any Attila or Alaric ever led, but a horde bent on the preservation of life, of decent life, not its destruction, a horde mobilised for civilisation – not, heaven forbid, as we know it, but of a new, sane, decent civilisation that is to come . . . It is not Rome we will sack, but the dreadful fortresses of our masters, places like the plant at The Hok, and its equally absurd partner across our polluted estuary, I mean that of EUREAC at Spartshaven . . .'

Again the cheers rolled up to her, funnelled by the fish market from the square outside and so right up to the dais – but again the flatness of the place ruined the effect for most of those there. Spread out beneath the dripping plane trees, the low cloud, they were cold and wet from the still-persistent drizzle, and each she and he heard only their own voices, a little hoarse, a little pathetic, and those of their neighbours: they had little sense of the unity of the rally that Catedratika Arendt was trying so hard to get them to share.

To Paul and Mik, now standing quite close to the flagstaffs at almost the furthest point from her, she seemed an absurdly distant and insignificant figure, bouncing above the heads of the crowd like a partially inflated bath toy – quite like, Mik thought, Flossie the Whale he had bought as a present for his niece. Absurd because the PA system was a good one when managed by an expert, so the voice that boomed over and around them seemed to belong to some latter-day Brunnhilde.

'. . . but for once, friends, I am not here to give you a

history lecture. Oh, yes. I know it's what many of you have come to expect from me, but today I am here because I was born here. Yes.' She flung out an arm. 'On a farm five kilometres out from St Romain, and my mother used to sell our surplus potatoes and onions right *there*' – the hand stabbed out, almost, Mik felt, at him, at the spot where he stood – 'and she bought good wholesome fish for us all, right *here*.

'Friends, my cousin-in-law sold that farm last year for one tenth of what it was worth twenty years ago, and she sold it because my cousin is dead. At thirty years old, of a rectal cancer that clawed its way in his lower bowel like a crab, condemned him to an end dreadful for its pain and humiliation.'

In the silence she had created, many could now hear the drip of rain in the leaves of the trees, the chirp of sparrows, but then Julia Arendt began quickly and methodically to outline with facts and figures the ecological and human disaster that goes by the name of The Hok. She listed and classified the daily crises within the plant, specified the failures in routines and supervision; then went on to describe how the few fishermen who still worked found monsters in their nets – fish two-headed, crabs whose claw limbs carried two pairs of pincers instead of one, white fish whose flesh was black. She talked of milk yields destroyed because of high iodine-131 content; of strontium-89 and -90 seeping from leaks in cooling tanks right down into the water table; of cats, moles and birds who freely cross the perimeter and of children who pick the blackberries near it and fall ill.

Her voice grew louder, became thick with passionate disgust. Near the back of the hall Argand watched her with total absorption, the reasons for his presence in the echoing hangar forgotten. His grandmother, like Arendt's mother, had been born into a peasant family, farming poor, wind-swept land a few kilometres up the coast from St Romain, so he remembered now summers spent exploring curlew-haunted dunes scented with thyme and heather which had seemed, after the tiny flat in the city, paradisiacal.

'In the City of Brabt, out of every thousand deaths one hundred and twenty-seven are from cancer. In the Province as a whole, one hundred and nineteen. In Quiller, twenty-five kilometres to the north from here, the figure is one hundred and sixty-three; in St Sebastian, the parish in which my cousin died, the figure is one hundred and seventy-two. Here in St Romain, one hundred and eighty-five. In Douarnain, the last inhabited village between here and The Hok, the figure would work out as two hundred and sixteen, over one in five. I say 'would work out' thus, but now in Douarnain there are only one hundred and twenty people left from a population of over six hundred fifteen years ago. These are terrible figures. One in five die of cancer, twice the rate of the Province as a whole. Why? Why? Why?'

The answers to that question were: so that Brabt's contribution to the Common Market grid would not depend on the radicalised coalminers of the Zar; so that enriched plutonium-239 would be readily available in Europe for the bombs, rockets, even shells, that the NATO high command now wished to make the key of defence strategy against – 'against, my friends, not nuclear attack from the Warsaw Pact, they have their long-range missiles as a deterrent against that, but against conventional aggression'. Not least the answer to 'why?' was: 'because to undo the whole complex, scientific and bureaucratic as well as industrial and military, will mean the bosses having to admit that they got it wrong, and these stiff-necked people who worship nothing but the golden calf can never, never admit they are wrong.'

While Argand, near the back of the fish market, both appreciated the completeness and aptness of the biblical reference and was near enough to feel the pull of Arendt's rhetoric, and so momentarily allowed his own deepest convictions to be pushed back a little in his mind, Focking, out in the square and near the flagstaffs, was less impressed. Not only was this crazy little woman blaspheming against the established order, she was using crazy old-fashioned language to do it. He looked around him, wondered if he could find another sausage sandwich without leaving the area he had been allotted. Most faces were tilted towards the speaker and lit dully by the reflected glow from the stage; raindrops glistened in hair, ran unnoticed down cheeks. But here and there one or two had turned away, were facing back towards the town hall. And yes, moving too, easing their way towards the memorial to his left. As the first of these mavericks in the crowd, a slim but tough-looking youth dressed in a cotton padded jacket, brushed past Focking, Arendt was reaching for her peroration.

'Friends, sisters, brothers, the first stage of our great movement has been achieved. Your presence here demonstrates that. We are a mass movement, and as such we can influence the course of history. But we will not do that simply by gathering together first here and then there, in St Romain, in Hyde Park, at La Hague in Cherbourg or at The Hok in Brabt. Now we must do more, now we must move into the political arena, for the decisions needed to halt the nuclear age, to halt the nuclear arms race and nuclear technology, are political ones. And, Comrades, such is our strength, here and throughout the length and breadth of our Province, that the politicians at last know of us, have seen us, and either fear us or come to woo us, and we should greet them as a bride greets her bridegroom, prepared and adorned as the New Jerusalem. Friends, welcome Walter Beck.'

This time the cheers did roll up into a momentum strong enough to convince not only those in the echoing hall but even those right out on the peripheries of the crowd in the square. On the stage Arendt's place was taken by a short, stocky man, with a high, almost bald dome of a head and a heavy moustache. He wore, as he always did, a workman's navy-blue donkey-jacket over a red roll-neck sweater. His stance was relaxed, legs apart, hands in the side pockets of the jacket, and he looked up into a far corner of the fish market with, those close enough could see, just the hint of a smile dimpling the corners of his wide mouth. He waited for the applause to die away, made no attempt to halt it.

His first sentences were quiet, low key, but placed surely for the PA system. 'Brothers, sisters, dear Julia has me wrong again. It's always the case. I don't come to you from the outside as a wooer – I stand here because I have always been here . . .' The applause began again, and this time one hand taken from his pocket swept it laconically to one side. '. . . I was indeed a socialist before I was against nuclear war, but only because I was a socialist before 6 August 1945. But I was a member of this movement before I was a politician – that is, before I gave up full-time union work on entering the Moot in 1969. Sisters and brothers, don't think of me as a prospective husband seeking a bride. The case is not like that. Rather, think of me as one of you' – louder now, the delivery quicker – 'who comes to you not seeking favours but bringing to you a great gift: the greatest available to the anti-nuclear movement in Brabt. This gift, my friends, is nothing less than the Reformed Socialist Par. . .' And this time the applause was the greatest yet, although for most of the hall it did not obscure the sudden storm of cat-calls, whistles and then actual missiles from the right of the stage; and simultaneously extra lights, many of them, lit up the echoing interior as if by magic – the television crews knew at last that they had something that would make the ten o'clock news.

Argand pushed his way a little nearer the front, unable to resist the temptation to see how it was working, and was thus that little bit further from the scene of the second and appallingly more effective disruption right at the end of the square.

Meanwhile, Focking had kept his eye on the man in a padded cotton jacket who had brushed past him. Now someone he could not quite see in the crowd made a step out of his hands and hoisted the lithe youth up the nearest of the flagpoles – he had taken off his jacket and his teeth were clenched on the grip of a broad-bladed knife. Almost all the crowd, even those near the flagpole, were still attending to Beck's opening sentences, but already a few had turned to watch as the young man – you could see now against the grey sky that his face was lined, looked older than his fit body suggested – neatly severed the lines that held the Union Jack. He crumpled the wet cloth into a ball and chucked it out into the crowd. Many applauded, but several booed, and others shouted remonstration and disapproval. The youth – if he was a youth – slithered nimbly down the pole and was momentarily submerged by the crowd around him. Focking, grim-faced, acting by reflex and forgetting why he was there, began to push towards the war memorial.

Up at the front Argand's plan was working well. A sudden charge, more a push than a charge, from a dozen beefy Rural Guards, unarmed according to his advice, had sent the twenty or so anarchists back into the void created by the removal of the stalls. They almost dropped through the gap, in the way a man stumbles when he finds that a step he was expecting has gone. No one seemed too bothered, least of all Beck. There go the anarchists, most seasoned rally attenders thought, and waited patiently for the real business of the meeting to be resumed.

At the back Focking was almost in time to catch the lean,

dark man, perhaps would have done had not another man, taller, fair, carrying the first man's coat, got in the way – deliberately, Focking thought, as he struggled in the press to get round him. Three agile heaves, his legs expertly knotted round the shaft, brought the first man up to the green, white and yellow tricolour of Brabt, with the arms of the Grand Duke set square in the middle of the white panel. The cheers and shouts of disapproval were far more marked this time – perhaps because Beck was no longer speaking. More jostling, then scuffles broke out, as again the knife glinted in the dull air, then more brightly as several photo flashes went off too. Again the sodden rectangle was balled up and thrown out over the upturned faces of the crowd. This time it unfolded itself in a slow explosion before drifting on to the raised hands below.

Focking loved his flag, you could say. Though it is doubtful if any emotion he felt was pure, untainted by the deep self-deceit which characterises such people. He knew, too, an offence had been committed. 'The Flag is the symbol of the State, and any attack on the Flag is an attack on the State . . .' are the words inscribed in Article 24 of the Brabanter Constitution (1812, revised 1919). He was a big man, a little out of condition, but speed was not what was needed to get to the foot of the flagpole before the vandal dropped down it.

With the weight of the bodies he had pushed through pressing on him again, with the noise, abuse, encouragement ringing in his ears, and his own voice bellowing that he was a police officer, Focking grabbed for the damp jeans as they came in reach, dodged the kick at his head he had been expecting, registered that the man's thighs were lean and hard, that he was faced with someone tough, not necessarily an easy adversary; then he grabbed at the man's arm as it came in reach, searching for the hold he could twist into a limb-breaking lock.

Tremp saw Focking fall, had been moving in from the left, was only ten metres away, but then was swept back as the crowd surged forward in panic. The town hall doors had been opened and State Security Troopers in full riot kit – visored helmets masked against gas, truncheons, shields – surged down the steps and across the road in a solid phalanx. CS gas canisters popped in the air ahead of them and fell trailing their noxious vapour behind them. And Beck's appeals for calm, for order, booming out through the fish market and over the square, went quite unheeded.

15

Focking's family lived on the twenty-fifth floor of a block of flats that had been built under a special scheme to provide Grade B2 accommodation for government employees who would not otherwise have been able to afford it. Only men with several years of loyal service need apply. There were twenty-eight floors in all. Three elevators served them but from a tower of their own, a narrow shaft set twenty metres from the block itself and linked to it on alternate floors by narrow, enclosed bridges.

Tremp, more than ten metres from the ground, suffered vertigo. Crossing the bridge at floor twenty-four was the Via Dolorosa for him, and he had his cross to bear too – the news for Dm Focking that her husband was dead.

Having negotiated the bridge without being sick, though still terrifyingly aware that, to get down, it had to be done again, he lurched up a short flight of stairs and groped along the open gallery to number 285. A boy about six years old, fat like his father, with hair as flame-coloured as Piet Focking's had been at that age, opened the door.

'Is your mother in?'

A voice from the kitchen answered, 'What is it?'

'I'm a police officer – a friend, colleague of Piet Focking. May I come in? May I speak to you alone?'

Perhaps Tremp's pallor – induced more by the horror of vertigo than the purpose of his visit – forewarned her. She shut the boy and girl, very similar in appearance and only fourteen months younger than her brother, into the lounge where a large colour television was already repeating an edited version of the day's events at St Romain. She was tubby, short, had straw-coloured hair, thickish spectacles, and was dressed in a padded nylon housecoat whose pattern and colours suggested the scales on a herring. She led him into a spotlessly clean dining room.

'All right then. He's dead. Is that it?'

Tremp turned to the uncurtained window. Far, far too far below him the River Flot bent round Wilhelmspark with its floodlit fairy castle, and so to the docks. Towering cumulus, its peaks still catching the gold of the setting sun, filled the east horizon as the rain moved on into Europe. Below, dusk was falling, the street lights already on, the bridges lit, the clockface over the Moot beaming like a full moon positioned sickeningly beneath him.

'Well . . . yes.'

'The silly, silly stupid bastard.'

He turned. She looked grim certainly, angry even, but distraught with grief, no. Her eyes fluked away to a heavy sideboard, mock something or other, Spanish perhaps, which supported the first four volumes of the sort of encyclopedia that is sold by instalments to those of us who wish our children to do well. There was a framed photograph above them – of Henry Hemeling, the collaborating head of Brabt's government during the Occupation.

'I suppose I should know how it happened. You'll want to tell me anyway.'

Tremp drew a deep breath. 'We can't be sure of all the details yet. But he was knifed. And died instantly. No pain. At St Romain. The anti-nuclear rally . . .'

A scream from the next room. Then angry shouting. 'Ma, ma, Elspeth's taken my machine pistol, she's taken my . . .'

While Focking's wife was out, Tremp, out of habit, looked

99

over the room he had been put in. Obviously it was not used often – at any rate the children were kept out of it. There was none of the scuffing, the fingermarks, the small toys left in corners that characterised what he had seen of the rest of the apartment. A room for guests, for formal occasions, and, judging from the desk by the window and the small bookcase in a corner, the room which Focking used as his study: the place where he would sit in the evening and take longer than he really needed writing up his report for the day, checking the household accounts.

On the top shelf of the bookcase – *Judaism: The Curse of Europe*, *The SS – What it Stood For* . . .

'I don't want to know.'

He turned from the books. Dm Focking was back, arms akimbo, spectacles glinting up at him.

'I don't want to know. Not now. He wasn't a bad man. Go now.'

'Well. Yes. But . . .'

'Piss off.'

The bridge across the dreadful gulf to the lifts.

'I'd like to say . . . he was a good man. I mean, I know. I worked with him . . .' Now, at last, he was remembering the guidelines set down for this situation by a social psychologist.

'Oh, for Christ's sake, go. Don't you see? The children. They have to go to bed.' She thumped the top of the side-board with a large red clenched fist.

As he went through the tiny hall, tripping on a toy tank, and so to the front door, Tremp heard, 'And later there will be a special report from St Romain, more details of what happened and comment from senior officials. But it does seem clear that amongst the fatalities was a police officer attached to the new bureau of . . .'

He turned.

'You'll be told, of course. I mean, how it happened. Meanwhile, if you're in difficulty or trouble . . . I mean, with money and so on, you must let us know.'

She opened the door. The TV announced that next of kin had been informed.

'The procedure is . . . later someone will come. I mean, from the clinic. So if there's anything you want, I'm sure, I know everyone will be most supportive.'

She shut the door and he was faced with the gallery and the bridge back to the lift.

Why the hell, Tremp asked himself, why the hell did I ever ask for a transfer from Crime. I was doing all right. I was. And now all *this*.

16

'First, a brief resumé of what actually happened at the moment of crisis. It seems that shortly after Walter Beck took the rostrum two disturbances broke out, perhaps independently, perhaps coordinated. All that has yet to be established.' The presenter of the weekend news magazine, a tall, bald man with an East European accent, stabbed at a simplified map of the town centre of St Romain. 'What is clear is that at the front of the hall, here, a group of anarchists began to heckle and throw tomatoes. This interruption had been anticipated and was, by all accounts, dealt with efficiently and with little fuss. But meanwhile *here* (another stab), a second and more sinister disturbance was under way. A man, assisted by an accomplice, climbed first one flagpole, then another, cutting down the flags. This apparently provoked heavy fighting between rival factions. Meanwhile, a plainclothes policeman moved in to arrest the vandals. He was knifed. To the heart. And died almost instantly.

'*Here*, in the town hall, all this had been observed by the officer in charge of a detachment of State Security Troopers, two hundred of them, in full riot gear. He it was who launched those troopers into the square.

'Hell on earth is how a Dutchman and his wife described it. We interviewed them just half an hour ago outside St Romain general hospital, casualty ward.

' "It was ridiculous, absurd. The Troopers just came at the rear of the crowd as if we were . . . as if we were blacks or something. No warning. No calls to disperse. Just straight in with batons and CS gas. I mean, there were many children in the rally. But the crucial thing was this. There was no way out. The crowd broke in front of the charge, but came against more police in the side streets, with water cannon and more gas. And they wouldn't let us through. It was hell. Hell on earth . . ."

'And that seems, at the moment, in advance of the official inquiry which Secretary Prinz has already announced, that seems to have been the principal cause of the tragedy which has encompassed so far four deaths as well as that of Detective Ensign Focking, six hundred admitted to hospital, though most now discharged, and over one thousand five hundred arrests, almost all of whom have now been released. We'll take a break there.'

Commercials for German Fords, French Renaults, Spanish wine. A public service announcement reminding guest workers who could no longer find employment that free travel vouchers to take them back to their countries of origin were available at all town halls.

'Welcome back to this night of tragedy, which will of course have political implications reaching far beyond the mere . . . purely human perspective we have so far considered. For instance, it is almost certainly significant that the incident that led to the death of Focking coincided with Deputy Prime Minister Walter Beck's speech from the platform, which was, of course, cut short. Its content was to have been of very considerable political importance and just an hour ago the following brief statement was put out from the Reformed Socialist headquarters in Jaurèsstras, City of Brabt.

' "Deputy Prime Minister Beck, on behalf of the coordinating committee of the Reformed Socialist Party of Brabt, confirms that his speech at The Hok anti-nuclear rally would have announced a new orientation between the Reformed Socialists and most of the smaller parties of the left, and also the anti-nuclear and ecological movements. However, it is possible that, in the light of events at The Hok and St Romain, details of this new orientation will have to be reconsidered. Consequently we are not able to give a fuller statement at this point in time."

'Well. There we are. Were we to hear of an alliance? A popular front? Or merely a statement of goodwill and shared intent between the various parties and organisations? I must say, one cannot help feeling that they are stalling because they are afraid that the significance of the announcement would be lost in the aftermath of today's events.

'One last footnote, an ironic one if you like. The Ministry of Internal Affairs has now confirmed that the murdered policeman, Detective Ensign Focking, was at the rally as an observer for the new and controversial Bureau of Advice and Investigation. And it has also confirmed that so far, within hours of the baton charge, the bureau has already received six hundred and thirty-two complaints relating to the police and particularly the State Security Troopers . . .'

Paul leaned forward and switched off. From the sofa, his legs pulled up, sucking the knuckle of one white thumb, Mik watched him. One eye was bruised and swelling.

'Well then. You were right. It was that Focking.'

Mik released his thumb. 'I told you,' he said. 'So, you see, I can be right about the other man too.'

Paul shrugged, went to the dented fridge. 'It doesn't follow. It doesn't follow at all. Do you want a beer?'

'All right.'

The fridge door had developed a creak from the battering it

had had, but the light still came on.

'It was dark here. And it was getting dark at St Romain. Gloomy anyway, with the weather.'

Mik sighed, looked out over the bare windowsill where the coloured glass poodles had been. They were going over ground they had already covered two or three times as they made their way back, first to the Aureole and then to their flat.

'It wasn't anything like dark. Just dull. I'm sure it was the same man. I'm sure about the teeth and I'm sure about the tattoo.'

Paul grimaced. 'Well, we've learnt our lesson. We want to keep out of all that sort of thing. You need a beer,' he said, and pulled off the ring tag. 'And we'll have a bit of that English cake I bought.'

PART THREE: INVESTIGATION

17

Sunday morning and the market square at St Romain
struggled to piece together normal life, work even, much like
a man with a four-bottle hangover. Jan Argand watched from
the balcony as municipal workers – elderly men for the most
part, dressed in black berets and blues – moved as if tranced
across the cracked flags, pushing huge brooms through
ankle-deep litter. Others forked the mounds into black
plastic bags, which were hoisted on to municipal pick-ups.
The fish market rang with the steady sound of hammering,
of dropped metal ties and the sharp percussion of planks,
magnified to the volume of pistol shots by the empty hall, as
the dais was dismantled. In the middle of it all, in spite of it
all, three large old ladies had set up their fish stalls, having
checked their wares for the evil misshapes which had given
their market such a bad name; and out in the open, near the
three flagpoles where Focking had died, four or five more
stood guard over lettuces, tomatoes, gladioli and carnations
which no one threatened to buy. The air was warm, but the
sky still cloudy. Out in the little harbour a high-prowed
inshore fishing boat was chugging out of the open sea past
the lighthouse.

At Argand's side the mayor, a portly little man, lit a
Gauloise behind cupped hands. 'That's it, you see,' he said.
'If they come in from local waters to catch the market, they
risk tipping monsters out of their holds, or worse still a spot
radiation check catches them over the mark. So they have to

109

go further off and come in late, and no one buys fish wholesale at half past nine in the morning. So now we have a fleet of four boats. Before The Hok, thirty-three . . .'

Argand found the man a nuisance and a bore. He was trying to piece together a picture of how the square must have looked to an observer on this balcony at the moment Focking was killed. He remembered well enough what it had been like down in the fish market, and it had been a salutary experience. Commissioner Argand, lately at Public Order, knew about crowds: how to count and limit them; how to split them, get them to disperse in the directions and at the speed the exigencies of the moment demanded. But he had not known much of what it is like to be part of one.

The first thing that had surprised him was that the sudden convulsion more than a hundred metres behind him had been communicated not directly but by a sudden shift in the physical feel of the people around him. What had been solid, unmoving, began suddenly to twist and eddy, and this uncertainty had been echoed in speech and cries. It seemed to him that in the past he had underestimated how quickly a crowd loses its psychological cohesion; psychically it disperses long before it comes apart physically. All of which was interesting, but not now the problem in hand.

'Jan,' Prinz had said to him on the phone late on Saturday evening, 'he was one of your men and I've talked it over with Piet Stent and we agree you are the man for the job. Of course, he'll put all the resources of Crime at your disposal but you are the man for the job, and I want you to make it your top priority.' For once, Argand had welcomed one of the Secretary's suggested irregularities. He had not liked Focking, but nevertheless his response to the murder was almost atavistic. It was always thus when one of his men was hurt or killed.

Glass shattered over to their left as workmen pulled the

broken shards of a shop window out on to the pavement. But Argand hardly heard, was striving again to visualise the moment. Eight press photographs – he had plates of them in his briefcase already – had been taken of the desecration of the flags and so, presumably, of Focking's killer, but all from low down, from a distance, and in a poor light. They were almost as contradictory as the statements that had so far been collected from eyewitnesses: brown or black hair, sallow complexion or unshaven. That he was fit and lithe all agreed – it could hardly have been otherwise. It's no easy matter to shin up a wet flagpole even with the help of flag-lines and a push up from . . . a girl, some said, a young man said others, you can't really be sure these days, can you?

'It's a vicious circle, you see,' the mayor was saying as he tossed his cigarette out over the pavement and into the road, 'the fish goes, so then the farm produce, and soon even the shops feel the pinch. And now EUROSHOP wants a hyper just off the Brabt–Antwerp motorway twenty kilometres away, and I should think that'll be the end of us.'

'Squadron Commandant Krater is in the council chamber. Could you ask him to come out here?'

'Squadron . . . oh yes. Yes, of course. I'll go and get him.'

While he waited, Argand walked slowly to each end of the short balcony, always with his eyes fixed on an imaginary circle drawn about one metre above the ground with a diameter of about four metres. Within that circle Focking had been stabbed; the wound had been made at that height above the ground, made in the thick of a dense crowd whose heads were one and a half and more . . .

'Commissioner?'

Argand turned. Krater stood to attention. He was in uniform, black, with black breeches above black boots, white and chrome accoutrements, buttons and badges, a round cloth hat, black-braided with a small peak, the whole distantly echoing the informal uniform of late nineteenth-century cavalry. In fact, the first State Security Troopers had been recruited from a disbanded regiment of mounted guards who had taken with them not only elements of the uniform but also a considerable amount of know-how and ethos. After all, since 1789, cavalry's role has had as much to do with the suppression of civil riot as with military reconnaissance and pursuit.

Krater was tall, well made, elegant even, with a duelling scar on one cheek and a cavalryman's moustache. Argand suspected that, had the practice not been declared illegal by the Popular Front government of 1937, he would have been *Van der* Krater.

'Commandant. I am trying to visualise what happened down there yesterday. Or to be more precise I am trying to visualise how it would have appeared to your observers up here on this balcony. Were you here?'

'Yes, Commissioner. Well. Yes and no. I'll explain.' This was said briskly, with no hint of the uncertainty the content of the words appeared to carry. 'I was here when the killer climbed the first flagpole and cut down the Union Jack. I then turned back into the council chamber, where a telephone link with Commissioner Wynand of the Rural Guard had been set up. I wanted to be certain that he knew what was happening. Unfortunately he could not answer. As you know, he had based himself in his Rural Guard headquarters behind this building and had contact with the rally itself only by radio and through the television cameras in the fish market. At that moment, he was directing, by radio, the operation against the anarchists and did not want to speak to me. Then one of my men called to me that something important was happening and I returned to this balcony. The killer had just thrown the Brabanter flag into the crowd and was slithering down the pole. I have good glasses, Zeiss

112

ten by fifty, and I could see Detective Ensign Focking pushing towards . . .'

'You knew Focking?'

'Yes. He was on this balcony with another of your men just before the rally opened. I found them here. He seemed very concerned about finding a beer somewhere before he attended your briefing.'

Argand nodded. 'What happened then?'

'Focking was almost near enough to grab him, the killer, perhaps two metres away, with only one or two people between them. As his feet reached head level, the killer lashed out, with his feet, forcing people to draw back. He dropped into the space he had created and moved off. As he did, Focking . . .'

'One moment.'

'Yes?'

'Just now you said you were called out of the council chamber by one of your men. Because "something important was happening". What was that?'

Krater looked confused, but openly so, as if the answer was self-evident. 'Why, the man had climbed the middle flag-pole. The one with the Brabanter flag on it.'

'Why was this important? I mean, it was surely predictable. I suppose he went for the Union Jack first to draw attention to himself. It was surely predictable that he would follow up with our flag.' Argand took a pace or two away, chewed on a thumbnail as he again stared down at the memorial. One of the workers was trying to decide whether or not to put a battered wreath of laurels back on it. Eventually they went into the pick-up. 'Your subordinate's report could not have been a surprise. Yet you gave up trying to speak to Wynand and came out in time to focus your glasses on what was happening, in time to see Focking moving in. Do I have that right?'

'Yes. Yes . . . that is how it was.' A gesture of dismissal, then with just a hint of the arrogance that betrayed his social origins: 'Oh come, Commissioner. You know how it is at such times. One's actions are never quite rational. If they appear to be, well, that's good luck rather than good judgement.'

Argand let the noises of repair and demolition reassert themselves between them. Then: 'Go on.'

'Go on?'

'What happened next?'

'The killer moved off.'

'In which direction?'

'Obliquely to the left. Away from us.'

'And Focking followed.'

'Yes.'

'So both had their backs to you. Did the man still have his knife out?'

'I imagine so.'

'Come, Commandant.'

'I did not see it.'

'Could you keep both in view in your glasses at the same time?'

'Yes. Well, perhaps momentarily no. But then Focking caught up with the man, pulled on his shoulder . . .'

'Which?'

'Left. I think. Twisted him about. Briefly I saw the man's face over Focking's shoulder. Then he stabbed Focking. Focking doubled over the blow and clutched at someone else near him before sinking to his knees. The killer was trying to get away, but was impeded . . . and at that moment, perhaps five, ten seconds after the blow, when it seemed apparent he would get away and a man down there, a policeman, was dying, I ordered the troopers out.'

'By pocket radio.'

'Yes, by pocket radio to the squadron commandant who was with the men in the quadrangle below.'

Again Argand screwed up his eyes in an effort to imagine the almost deserted square below filled with a dense crowd, packed tight, men, women, and children too, pushing, shoving, heaving to and fro, then not the whole scene but a tiny part of it brought into focus by a pair of Zeiss ten by fiftys.

'Did you actually see the blow? Did you see the knife go in?'

Krater was silent.

'Well?'

'No.'

'I should not have believed you if you had said otherwise. But your report immediately after asserts that you did.'

'I don't see where this is leading. I thought Focking had been stabbed, probably to death. One has had experience of such things, and the man had a knife. And I was right. It is immaterial whether or not I actually saw the knife go in.'

'Nevertheless you said you had seen just that. And now you deny it.'

'But so what? You're wrong anyway to say that I said I saw the knife go in. I said I saw a man stabbed, and in that I was precisely right.'

The insolence had returned. Krater's voice rose a tone or two – triumph was hinted at.

'I think,' said Argand, meditatively it seemed, 'I think, if I had been you, I should have said that I *thought* I had seen a man stabbed.' He straightened, his voice became a touch lighter, almost friendly. 'Well, from what you say, you had the man's face, in focus, in a pair of strong binoculars. What did he look like?'

Krater let out a breath, almost a sigh.

'Really, I thought that is what you had come to ask me,

115

although that is in my report too. He was fair, fair-skinned, brownish hair receding a little, cut short but not very short. About twenty to twenty-five. A thin sort of face, with heavy eyebrows. About one metre eighty. Seventy kilos. He was dressed in a fisherman's sweater, jeans, tennis shoes . . .'

'Other testimony does not agree with that in every particular. One of the press pictures at least suggests he was darker than you say.'

Krater shrugged. 'It was a bad light. There was much confusion. But I am prepared to stand by and swear to my description.'

'Could you pick his photo out from a selection?'

'Yes. I think so. Unless the selection contained several closely resembling him.'

'One last question. The squadron commandant in the quadrangle logged your order to move his troopers out, deployed as for a baton charge, at fifteen forty-two precisely. Do you accept that?'

'Yes. Why not? I didn't log it myself until later, and I then had to estimate the time. I put it at fifteen forty-five, but if Rizler says fifteen forty-two then I am sure he is right.'

18

Argand's inquiries in St Romain took up the rest of the day but yielded little; it was not until late on Monday morning that he was able to set out back to Brabt. On the motorway Argand considered again Squadron Commandant Krater and his evidence.

Krater was a type he disliked and had learned to distrust. They were survivals from earlier times, petty nobility, small landowners: all had kept the junker mentality, though the cleverer ones now dominated the professions or had safely transferred their assets into industry. The less clever muddled along – their estates mortgaged, their connections in areas of influence dwindling, and their sons forced to earn a living. With the army cut back to the Mobile Operations Unit, a brigade of guards and two armoured divisions committed to NATO, it was not unusual for them to enter the police, and with its flavour of cavalry still lingering they usually chose State Security.

Nevertheless, Argand thought, Krater, though arrogant, was not necessarily at fault. His statements did conflict, but only in minor ways; he had acted hastily, perhaps made an error of judgement, but the circumstances had been confused, and that was Wynand's fault as much as anyone's. On the other hand . . . well, there were other statements to check, film, photographs and television. Until he had been through the lot, he would reserve judgement – not that judging Krater was any of his business.

As the car sped past the first residential areas, shoddy high-rises built on reclaimed mudflats, vandalised and dirty, the homes of guest workers, he turned to the file that had been handed to him as he left St Romain town hall.

It had been prepared at the Ministry and taken out by motorbike to catch him there, and there was a minute in Prinz's own hand covering it:

'Jan. This is the first batch of complaints against police action on Saturday that we have had time to process. Don't bother too much with them now, getting Focking's killer is your top priority. A statement is to be put out saying that all action on complaints is to be held back until the commission of inquiry has made its preliminary report. That will hold them. However, I am passing them on to you as you may find leads in your hunt. Apropos of which there do seem to be indications that members of the League of Marxist–Leninist Militants were near the flagpoles.

'I would like you to look at just one complaint for its own sake. It's from Catedratika Julia Arendt, Dean-elect. She has quite a lot of pull these days, so perhaps you should see her, just a courtesy visit. Handled by you with all your usual skill, she might also offer a lead on 2LM and similar sects. W.P.'

The informality, chumminess of this irritated Argand. He had worked for Prinz for too long, had been betrayed by him too often. The worst thing about it was that it revealed utter incomprehension of what really did motivate Argand to undertake tedious, often unpleasant, occasionally dangerous, and often downright hideous, work. The file on his knees forgotten, he lifted his head and gazed abstractly out over his driver's shoulder at the brutal curves of the motorway and the steady flow of traffic thundering along it. They had left the spur that leads to The Hok, were now on the short stretch of the Antwerp–Brabt autoroute that took them through the now thickening and older suburbs. Duty.

Loyalty. To what? To all that is right, good, just. But how to define these? Argand shook his head. Such uncertainties were no longer unfamiliar and they bothered him deeply, made him feel insecure, angry . . .

'My God, there are still some stupid louts around.' Bert Jenks, his driver, an ex-sergeant from Public Order supplementing his pension, nodded upwards indicating something behind. Argand shifted his position, saw in the rear-view mirror the grille of a truck far too close to them. He turned, took in the word *Berliet* just as it pulled into the fast lane, began to overtake them. He had no time to get a clear picture of the driver, who was now on the far side, but there was a passenger, fair, thin-faced – that was about all he could take in.

'He's well over the limit for laden vehicles.'

'We'll take his number when he pulls in. Report him,' said Argand grimly. He looked up at two rows of orange gas cylinders, stacked horizontally, held in place with chains. Side winds momentarily buffeted them, then Jenks had to brake with an oath as the truck pulled in in front of him far too soon. A Mercedes tore by in the fast lane, lights on, horn blaring, perhaps that was why . . .

Then it happened. First one chain then another whipped up into the air like snakes, and the cylinders, each about a metre long and a decimetre or so in diameter, began to turn on each other, nudging, trundling each other towards the lip. Jenks saw the danger, sounded his horn, flashed lights, then swung the official black Peugeot into the slow lane. Sickeningly the truck echoed the manoeuvre, pulled in with him, almost as if they were a display team moving in formation. The first cylinder dropped, hit concrete with sparks, bounced well over a metre high, and swinging on its own axis caught the off-side wing of the Peugeot. It glanced off, hurtled across the path of a large bus and finally smashed into the crash barrier. With the off-side tyre squealing in protest at the metal thus savagely clamped on it, Jenks's efforts to pull the car on to the hard shoulder were futile; and the next cylinder was poised like a diver on the edge, but miraculously it rolled back, for the truck, like the Peugeot, was now braking sharply. Then the Peugeot's tyre burst – Jenks corrected the first lurch out into the middle lane that followed and forced the freed steering mechanism to pull the sagging car first on to the hard shoulder and then through a low and not substantial rail at the foot of the last grass embankment before Brabt. Again the truck seemed to follow or go with them, but this time it accelerated. Six more cylinders tumbled in quick jangling succession but the momentum had gone; there was not enough speed to throw them as high as the first, and the only one that actually hit the Peugeot thudded into the driver's door with a savage enough clang but never looked like causing the sort of damage the first had been capable of, never looked like crashing through the windscreen, killing or maiming in quite hideous ways both driver and passenger . . .

Unless, thought Argand, it explodes.

It did not. Nor indeed did any of them. All were empty. But they caused havoc enough. The coach had accelerated out of trouble round the truck when it slowed, but six other vehicles were damaged, two were write-offs, and five people were taken to hospital, where one died four days later without recovering consciousness.

19

'I suppose, Commissioner, I should feel honoured.'

Argand glanced round the large room Julia Arendt had shown him into. It was unexpected: not simply as a workplace in what he knew to be her home, but because it did not match his expectations of what an academic in one of the humanities needs in order to do her job. There were certainly books, thousands of them on white shelves; there were papers set out with methodical untidiness on a large desk. But there were also modern filing systems; a visual-display unit with wallets of microfiches and spools of microfilm; what looked like a small computer terminal; piles of documents with celluloid tapes sticking out of them; extremely complex charts on the walls; and other gadgets whose purposes he did not know. One turned out to be a coffee machine which the Catedratika set briskly into operation.

'Honoured? Why?'

Arendt did not smile. She rarely did and when it came it was a blessing – like sun over well-hedged farmland and copses after rain. But generally she was severe – intense, animated, energetic, but severe. She wore now a suede sleeveless waistcoat over a light woollen jumper, and old-fashioned slacks cut rather fulsomely to make the best of a spreading waist and behind. A pair of spectacles hung from a silk cord and rested on her large chest. Had not her small, well-boned and well-lined face with its penetrating and serious eyes, its rather thin and unpainted mouth declared that comfort was something she would dispense rarely and only when absolutely necessary, her appearance might have suggested the word 'motherly'. In short, she reminded Argand of her, and his, forbears – land-holding peasants whose survival through centuries had depended on efficient and unrelenting control of their environment.

'Your office has put out a statement. Complaints about police misconduct at The Hok and St Romain will not be processed until the official commission of inquiry has made its first reports.'

'That does not in the least mean that we are not ready to receive them, nor that they will be shelved.'

Large eyebrows rose. 'No? I must say you surprise me. No. Don't look angry. You have a reputation for honest thoroughness exceptional in one of your eminence. However, I am a historian, and my special field has been popular protest.' She gestured over the room. 'You won't find a single case in all this where complaints of police brutality have been speedily investigated and acted on. Though many, many instances of pious resolutions.'

She poured coffee and as they manipulated cups, sugar and so on, Argand asked her why she wanted to see him. She explained, while clearing a pile of photocopied nineteenth-century fly-posters from a high-backed wooden chair for him and putting herself in her adjustable office chair, that before she entered her complaints she wished to be sure she was using the correct procedures.

'Nothing, both in my experience as a historian and as an activist myself, is so often used to delay the proper examination of such things as the use of procedural devices. "We most deeply sympathise with your tragic situation but regret nothing can be done since your letter of the first of last month is addressed not in triplicate but in duplicate to the Lord

High So and So whereas it should have been sent to His Egregriousness the Pomposity of this and that." Commissioner, I am going to throw the book at you, and I want to do it properly.'

Hackles rising again, Argand protested that in the eight weeks since his bureau had opened every complaint had been looked into within twenty-four hours, and if progress thereafter had not been as quick as he . . .

'But this is rather different. The wife of a businessman insulted by a traffic policeman, a trade union official jostled on a picket line . . . I am talking about two or three thousand people assaulted, nearly two thousand arrested without cause, very considerable damage to property both privately and corporately owned.'

Could an individual lodge a complaint on behalf of other individuals? Yes – but only with their written consent, or that of their guardians if they were minors or disabled. Could an organisation complain on behalf of individuals? Yes, the first proviso remained and to it were added others. The individuals would have to be members and acting at the time of the incident as members of the organisation; an organisation could also act where it existed to protect or represent the interests of its members: thus, say, a charity concerned with the welfare of the deaf could pursue a complaint on behalf of a deaf man.

Catedratika Arendt pushed on. 'Can an organisation complain of police action directed against not any of its individual members but against itself, as a corporate body?'

'Technically, yes. But the provision was set up with companies in mind where, for instance, a fraud investigation might be under way.'

In the end, as he expected she would, she found his answers unsatisfactory, though at least, she declared, not evasive. On the whole it seemed, they both agreed, that complaints issued by the Alliance of Professional and Technical Staff Against Nuclear Technology on behalf of its members might get by, but the fact was that its actual membership, as opposed to those who wore its badges and attended its rallies, was quite small. And most of it had been near the dais if not actually on it and well away from the baton charge. APTSANT would not be able to act for the thousands of unaffiliated demonstrators.

She offered him more coffee, and was a shade surprised when he accepted.

'I think it possible you now might be able to give me assistance.'

She waited, head on one side, alert but not suspicious or even wary. 'Really? How?'

'You know that, just before the State Security Troopers charged, a police officer, Detective Ensign Focking, was stabbed to death near the back of the crowd. Because he was working for my bureau, I have been asked to lead the investigation. Now it seems virtually certain that the killer was the man who cut down the flags and so cut short Walter Beck's speech. He is therefore someone who has done your cause harm, and in discovering this murderer and bringing him to book, our interests . . .'

'Commissioner,' Julia's voice and appearance were now very severe indeed. 'I can assure you that, whatever you think of me, my beliefs and so on, I remain entirely convinced that all murderers should be brought to book and it is the duty of us all to assist the police in such cases. God knows, there are not many of your activities left that I approve, but detecting and arresting murderers is one of them.'

Argand was abashed, drank coffee and replaced his cup on the corner of the desk to conceal his discomfort; then took a deep breath.

124

'There are indications that the man who cut down the flag was a member of an extreme left-wing group. The League of Marxist–Leninist Militants has been suggested. Now, we have a large file on them but what is not clear from it is their relations with the anti-nuclear movement and the Reformed Socialists. In particular, what their position is in Beck's proposed alliance. For instance, if . . .'

'I take the point. If they are to have a place in the alliance, then disruption of Beck's speech would be downright silly. Well, this is really quite interesting. Walter's attempts to get together what is in effect a new popular front – though he is avoiding the term – have of course been bedevilled by endless bickering between factions, and the case of 2LM is a case in point. I don't know how much you know about 2LM, but it is even more schizophrenic than most similar organisations. On the one side it has, or until quite recently did appear to have, quite considerable proletarian support, particularly in EUREAC and TULIP. In both, shop stewards' combines were 2LM-based – that is, the convenors were members and used 2LM's infrastructure to write, reproduce and distribute pamphlets, halls were hired in its name, and so on.

'But Beck's growing popularity, the general move to the left of the Reformed Socialists and the trades unions and the first steps towards democratisation of both have definitely undermined 2LM in that area. The recession hasn't helped either. EUREAC particularly is using redundancies to weed out what they call troublemakers. For both these reasons, militants and near-militants have been returning to the larger institutions.

'That's one side of 2LM. The other side is the student side. Most actual members are students, or recent graduates still unemployed – our own variety of *Berufsverbot* has ensured that. They provide the organisational infrastructure

I was talking about – the people with time to write, print and distribute pamphlets, knock on doors, get working people to meetings, sell the paper on the streets, and so on. Such people often have unconventional lifestyles and that side of 2LM was even more extreme than most. Wait a moment. You know about this yourself. That business at Brichtzee was investigated by your bureau and I must say you came out of it rather well. And of course you will know that a leading figure is a member of the Arts Faculty, Licentiate Petersen of the Law Department.

'The thing is this.' She was not exactly lecturing, rather introducing a seminar, laying down guidelines for discussion. It was said, Argand remembered, that, with her as Dean, formal lectures would be abandoned, a proposition which seemed to him to smack of . . . 'The thing is that, five months ago, when the groundwork for the alliance was being done, 2LM were definitely there. But, as the old party and union bosses realised that with Beck it was a case of if you can't beat him, join him, they came in too. I think it was the executive of the railway union who actually made it a condition of their cooperation that 2LM should be expelled. On the Wednesday before the rally, Walter dropped 2LM. And a couple of overtly Trot sects as well. So. Yes. I am forced to say that they did have good reason for disrupting Walter – or rather, not good reason, but credible motives based on malice.'

She swung her chair round, looked out of the large window over the trees and park that separated her house – set in what in the nineteenth century had been a bourgeois suburb, was now largely taken over by academics – at the blocks and rectangles that constituted most of the recently rebuilt university.

For a moment she fiddled with the wings of her spectacles, then she turned back.

'But you know, Commissioner, I don't like it. It's not their style. The flags perhaps, but not knifing a policeman to evade arrest. I should have expected a 2LM member to have brawled with your man certainly, to have simulated pain, bellowed, made as much fuss as possible. But a knife, and then slipping away . . .'

Argand stood up. 'Still. The League had no reason to respect Beck on Saturday and very probably they were planning a disturbance. Thank you, Catedratika, for clearing that up for me, and indeed for a helpful piece of background. You have no idea how sets of facts may be presented in our official files in one way and by people of your sort, if I may so put it, in a quite different light . . .'

She interrupted with a laugh. 'But, Commissioner, I have *every* idea. Much of my life's work has been devoted to bringing such contradictions into focus, and establishing how they condition and reinforce attitudes . . .'

'Well, anyway. It's been refreshing and useful to me to listen to you.'

At last the smile began to dimple her cheeks, into which a touch of pink was also spreading. At the door Argand turned. Over the large, old-fashioned mantelpiece was a landscape framed in white and grey with touches of gold. It represented a long sweep of shore with yellow sands and dunes with coarse grass. Three fifths of the picture was sky. On coming in, Argand's first reaction had been to reject it – it was too smudgy, too indistinct, the colours too vivid and varied. But now, perhaps because he was arrested at just the right distance, or because the light in the room had subtly altered, it brought back to him those three or four summers spent on his grandmother's smallholding.

Impulsively he turned, found Arendt closer to him than he had expected – she had followed him to the door.

'You mentioned in your speech on Saturday that your

family came from the coast near St Romain. Well. So did my mother's.'

'And the painting brought it to mind. It's very good, isn't it? Walter Sickert, an Englishman who belonged to the French School, painted it. He spent a summer on . . . our coast.' The smile was quite unqualified now. Argand was not sure which bewitched him more, it or the painting. 'My father-in-law was an art dealer. He gave it to us as a wedding present.'

Her hand was warm and dry. The temptation to return the very slight pressure she offered was great. But Argand was a grand master at resisting temptation.

20

Brian Tremp, brisk and dapper, went about his boss's business. He wore a slightly heavier suit of English cut, made from a composite fabric woven in Taiwan – for it was now September and, though the weather was clear, there was a chill on the air in the mornings and fog along the North Sea coasts.

He was back at Brichtzee, but this time walking through a featureless warren of small grey terraced cottages clustering round the now largely run-down railway yards at the back of the town. He found the house he wanted: a low door, three windows, two up, one down, all with grey shutters whose wood was rotten and whose metal fittings were rusted.

Eric Lanning himself opened the door. Tremp recognised instantly the young fat man, with his owlish spectacles and lank brown hair. Lanning recognised him too.

'Jesus. What do you want? I thought I'd finished with you.'

'May I come in?'

'Can I stop you?'

Lanning showed him through a tiny dark hall cluttered with all sorts of rubbish including a moped – one of its pedals snagged Tremp's leg and he wondered in the gloom if it had marked his trousers. The kitchen was filthy, dark and comfortless, filled with ancient household appliances, a mangle, dust-encrusted bottling jars, and so on, competing for space with piles of dusty crockery and almost empty bottles. On the old, and now obviously never used, cooking range a double gas ring was fed by orange rubber tubing from a butane gas cylinder.

'You'd better sit down.' Lanning gestured at a cane-bottomed chair – the cane of course was sagging. Tremp contrived to get most of his weight on the frame. 'My sister's out at work. My mother's been in bed for four years' – he jerked his head upwards – 'so she won't disturb us. What do you want now?'

Tremp looked round. It seemed extraordinary now to think that Argand and he had speculated whether or not Lanning was a V-man, an infiltrator planted in 2LM by Gapp.

'Nothing much,' he began. 'Just a few more questions about the League of Marxist–Leninist Militants.'

'I don't go with them no more.'

'No. I know you don't. They let you down really, didn't they?'

This was the right note to strike. Tremp had considered asking the Rural Guard to bring Lanning in, soften him up with solitary confinement for five or six hours, cryptic threats, a little 'jostling', but in the end he had decided on the soft approach.

'You could say that. Load of talk mostly. Bullshit mostly.'

'You didn't actually belong to the commune, did you?'

'You mean live in that dump with no clothes on? Not likely. But I went along to their what they called consciousness-raising sessions most days, had meals there and helped them with the building. I'm a joiner, see. Skilled.' He held out his hands, broad, strong, dirty, turned them over and looked at them. 'Been no work for three years now. So when they said they needed a joiner I went along. Couldn't take their food though. All beans and lentils, gave me gut-ache. Made me fart. Mam' – head jerked up to the ceiling again – 'says I went to gawk at bums and tits, but after the first day, well, you got used to it like. They were mostly scrawny anyway, not worth a second look with clothes on, and not really without neither. Except that Lisa Smit that went with the old feller Petersen. And they didn't mix much with the rest, him and his piano playing. Would you like a beer?'

Tremp agreed that he would. Lanning poured cheap sudsy stuff from an already opened litre bottle into cracked mugs.

Bit by bit Tremp pieced together something of the strains and tensions that had existed within the Hotel Bristol commune. Lanning was no fool, and no doubt the experience had been intriguing, entertaining, something quite out of the ordinary in the drab world of long-term unemployment in the least attractive area of a decaying seaside town. At all events he had kept his ears and eyes open, and not just for bums and tits.

There had been factions within the commune, that was for sure. Softies and hard-liners. Koonig had been leader – in so far as they went in for leaders, which wasn't much – of the softies, the majority. They talked a lot, smoked pot, were scrupulous about their whole-food diet, and spent a lot of time out, with clothes on, canvassing the poorer districts. Which was how they had found Lanning.

But then the hard-liners turned up. Not long after the first Rural Guard raid. There were only three of them: Hans Braun, who had given evidence at the inquiry about Koonig's fall downstairs, he was their leader – tall, thin, fit, fair hair and nasty blue eyes that looked loony – and two dark-haired brothers called Mark and Seb. Lanning didn't know their second name. They didn't go out much, bullied the others, and at the teach-ins they talked far more about revolution, killing, and that sort of thing . . . here Lanning became vague. He began to fidget too, his fingers twiddling

131

with an old but complex corkscrew, his eyes flitting away from Tremp's whenever they made contact.

'That lot weren't too careful about the law,' suggested Tremp. 'I mean, if you're all for the overthrow of everything, you're not going to be fussy about the odd bit of theft, illegal possession of weapons . . .'

Lanning gulped, turned owlish spectacles, which in the gloom of the filthy kitchen seemed almost to glow, full on Tremp's face.

'That's what this is about, isn't it? That's why you come here.'

The bite was so unexpected that Tremp for a moment did not know what to do: whether to play out more line, or strike. He held Lanning's gaze, and behind his own expressionless eyes his mind raced. Weapons. Three raids and none found. A joiner. He struck.

'You'd better come along with me now and show me where they were hidden.'

Which took a lot longer than it should have done, since the Hotel Bristol had been not just locked up but boarded up too, and the agent who handled it refused to open it without permission of the owners – a holding company with offices in Brabt, whose answering service said that everyone was on holiday – or a warrant. Recollecting the awfulness of Vustouk, the magistrate who could issue one, and conscious of the fact that the discovery of a cache which might or might not have held weapons was probably not going to forward the detection of Focking's killer – since presumably a perfectly ordinary sheath-knife had been used – Tremp began to wonder if he had not wasted a day.

Fortunately, His Serenity respected Argand, had quite taken to Tremp during the inquiry, and, like Catedratika Arendt, deplored the murder of policemen. Though woken out of a post-prandial nap, he signed the warrant without demur. It took another hour to round up the two carpenters the Rural Guard paid a retainer to for such jobs, and then another hour to get back to the Bristol and break their way in.

When it was all over, there was not much to see. Lanning led Tremp through the dark echoing hall, the dining room where the white piano still stood, upstairs to the third floor. The joiner opened shutters that looked out on to the sea, let in the cool light of late afternoon in early autumn, and then opened the fitted cupboard. He lifted a floorboard, found a catch beneath it and then lifted out the back. Although apparently made of six planks, it came out in one piece, revealing a space behind about half a metre deep, two metres high, one and a half across. It was, of course, empty.

'Neat eh? I done a good job on that.'

Had they chosen the place? No, Lanning chose it. They told him how they wanted it. Gave him measurements? Not exactly, showed him the stuff that was to go into it.

Which was what?

Although Lanning had presumably done his eighteen months' state service, including basic military training, he seemed surprisingly ignorant of modern small arms. It was only down at the Rural Guard headquarters, with the aid of an instructor who had only recently left the army, that they had been able to piece together what Lanning had been required to hide. It had all been wrapped or crated, but in its makers' original packing. By late evening they had agreed that the missing cache had probably included two hand-held launchers for the American heat-homing anti-aircraft missile known as Red-eye, and ten missiles. These standing upright had filled two thirds of the space. In the area left there had been a case of M26 grenades – the notorious anti-personnel bomb used in Vietnam – and four Beretta M12 sub-machine-guns with a wooden crate of one thousand 9-mm Parabellum to go with them. There remained the question of where they had come from: on the face of it a virtually impossible question to answer quickly without the actual weapons to hand. Not only are they all popular with terrorists, they are also standard equipment for most NATO infantry units, though the Heckler and Koch MP5 is more common than the Beretta. Even so, all are stockpiled in considerable quantities in hundreds of dumps, from Rotterdam to Mulhouse, from Namur to Kassel. However, Lanning had noticed a stencil on the box of grenades which someone had been at pains to paint out, but the outline still showed through. A red dagger, he said, and the motto 'Greater Love Hath . . .'

'I know,' the arms instructor filled in, 'MOBOP. And they do use Berettas.'

'That's right,' said Eric Lanning. 'When I was a kid, I always wanted to be one of them. But my eyes weren't right.'

And you were too bloody fat, thought Tremp.

Yet Lanning, the only connection of the commune Tremp had so far been able to trace, had been useful. Through him he had discovered what three previous raids could not manage: clear evidence that there was a far more sinister side to the commune and 2LM than their public image of pot-smoking nudists suggested.

He reported to Argand by phone. Half an hour later Argand rang back. Tremp was to get together a forensically equipped team of searchers, using Rural Guard and Crime, and return to the Hotel Bristol – this time taking every room apart, examining every particle of dust throughout the building. Meanwhile, he hoped to organise a task force, coordinating the resources of Crime, Rural Guards and State Security, to trace the missing weapons and also the elusive members, past or present, of the League.

21

'I should like to see you alone for ten minutes or so during the course of the morning.'

Argand, hanging his coat and hat on the old-fashioned horned stand he had imported into his brashly modern office, was brought up short. He turned. Petra Madjen was standing at the corner of his desk, as she did every morning when she brought in the agenda for the day and the first communications received.

'You have no appointment until eleven o'clock. Perhaps I could speak to you when you have seen the mail.'

'Of course, Dm Madjen. I'll buzz for you as soon as I'm ready.'

She nodded her head jerkily, her way of signifying satisfaction with an arrangement. Her sensible rubber-soled heels squeaked on the vinyl floor and she went, leaving behind the rather sweet odour of the English lavender water she used. For a moment Argand felt, as he had increasingly over the previous weeks, a tiny response of unaccustomed warmth somewhere quite deep inside him. She was so efficient, so thorough, yet so properly self-effacing, so *good*, so, it has to be faced, utterly unlike his wife.

He turned to the papers she had left. On the top were three reports relating to the motorway incident. The first was technical, summarised the actual sequence of events, the movements of the vehicles, the damage done. It ended significantly enough: the chains which secured, or failed to secure, the gas cylinders were fastened to a stanchion behind the cab by two marlin spikes; these in turn were attached to the bodywork by short chains, but each also had a long cord threaded through the eye, and the driver, whose name was Jakob Braun, was unable to explain why. It was just possible that with the other ends of these cords in his cab he had been able to jerk out the spikes without leaving it or halting the truck.

The Berliet had crashed into the toll barrier one kilometre on at the end of the motorway. The second document set out the charges laid: careless driving likely to endanger life; failure to secure a load properly; offensive and uncooperative behaviour, and so on. More than enough to hold him on remand for a week pending completion of inquiries.

The third was a report on Jakob Braun himself. He was the owner of a small campsite in the dunes not far from St Romain. After a bad season he was heavily in debt. He had two convictions for brawling and had been under a state psychiatrist. He drank and beat his wife and children. In a lean-to shed outside his house, which was a cabin constructed between two derelict railway carriages, he kept a collection of Nazi and fascist memorabilia.

Braun claimed that, that morning, he had received a final demand from the electricity company. To pay it, he had collected up all his empty gas cylinders, on each of which there was a returnable deposit, and was taking them into Brabt when the accident occurred. He had been in a temper about it, knowing that in the spring he would need the cylinders again and would have to pay far more for them than he was now claiming back. He admitted that because of this he might have been careless about securing the load.

None of which explained why he had in the inside pocket of his cracked leather jacket one hundred thousand gelds in old notes.

A covering note from the Traffic Commissioner said that, in view of the inconsistencies in Braun's statements, the cords on the marlin spikes and various other factors, he could not rule out the possibility that the spikes had been removed intentionally. He had therefore passed the file (copy to Commissioner Argand) to Commissioner Piet Stent of the Crime Bureau.

Argand sat hunched forward in his chair, eyes unfocused, living again the spinning, slowly turning orange cylinder as it clanged on the road before rising towards the windscreen, only to be deflected by the off-side wing. Then, before that, the truck almost nudging their rear fender, seen first in the mirror, then over his shoulder . . . but there had been a passenger, someone in the right-hand side of the cab. He pressed the bridge of his large nose with thumb and fore-finger, shook his head. But why no mention of him in anyone's report of the actual incident? Had Argand himself mentioned a passenger afterwards? He couldn't remember, couldn't be sure. He had been badly shaken and also con-scious of the day's work still not finished; probably he had forgotten him. And it would have been easy enough for the passenger to walk away from the toll barrier, or he might have been dropped earlier.

He buzzed his intercom. 'Get me Commissioner Stent's office, please. As quickly as you can.' While he waited for the call to come through, he became conscious that his reaction to knowing now that the accident had been no accident but a peculiarly nasty attempt on his life was that he had gone cold, quite cold, all over.

Stent was out. Argand left a message – that there had been a passenger in the Berliet truck, and he described him as well as he could. Then he tried to push it all out of his mind as he reached for the next folder. Yet something still nagged him.

Braun. Common enough, to be sure. Yet he felt that he had met it in the last month or so amongst the, what five hundred, six hundred other names that had come and gone.

Ministry of Internal Affairs, Department of Forensic Science. Report of an Autopsy conducted on Detective Ensign Piet Focking. With practised eye, Argand skimmed over the opening paragraphs – time of admission, clothes worn, temperatures, and so on, estimated time of death. Description of body – weight, height, build, general health.

Injuries, major: subject had been stabbed two inches below his left shoulder blade, the point entering the left ventricle . . . the wound was probably made by a narrow-bladed knife, double-edged, with a very sharp point.

Below his left shoulder blade. But Krater had said that Focking had doubled over the blow. What did this mean? That Krater believed Focking had been stabbed from the front. And he had seen the incident through his binoculars – though not the knife actually going in. Well, Krater's statements had been characterised throughout by a dogmatism which had already been shown to conceal uncertainty over several factors. Not only the blow, but the actual timing . . .

The odd thing was that he would have been more likely (though by no means certain) to have seen the actual stabbing if it had come from behind.

And then there was the wound itself. Not made by a broad sheath-knife with a serrated edge on one side but a longer affair, narrower, almost a stiletto. What it all added up to, on the face of it, was that Focking had not after all been killed by the man who had cut down the flags but by someone else, possibly, presumably, an accomplice. Did this make any difference to the inquiry? Not really. It was already well established that members of 2LM were in the crowd near the flagstaffs; there was no reason why his team and Stent's as well should not go on searching them all out, why experts should not continue trying to identify the man on the flagpoles from the press photographs, and of course every reason for redoubling appeals to the public for eyewitnesses to come forward.

The next three sheets were also stapled together with a Ministry of Internal Affairs heading. Argand was interested but perfunctorily so. Had he still been Commissioner for Public Order they would have concerned him very much indeed.

The General Secretary of the Reformed Socialist Party desired to hold a march and rally on Saturday, 12 September. The assembly points would be on the university campus; the march would go down Academikstras, via so and so, round this platz and into the next, down Wilhelm IX Boulevard, across St Sebastian Bridge and so into Wilhelmspark, where the final rally would be held; Deputy Prime Minister Walter Beck would give a speech at about three o'clock and that would be that.

The speech he had not been able to finish at St Romain.

Argand thought, the date is well-chosen. The following Monday is registration and enrolment day – the students will be back in town, as indeed will most of the workforce. The Moot reassembles on Thursday, 1 October, and that will open Beck's campaign to destroy the coalition with the PBDC and force an early election. Argand looked over it all in more detail, pencilled in one or two notes about the route – Commissioner Pranck had no false pride about accepting his predecessor's advice – and put it in the pending tray.

What else? A digest of the secret files on Julia Arendt. Why had he asked for that? He fidgeted for a moment, came as near to blushing as a man can who has not blushed for decades, checked that she had, as he thought, been a widow for fifteen years, and pushed it too into pending.

That seemed to be that. Except Petra Madjen wanted to see him. She had seemed concerned. Disturbed even. He pressed his buzzer.

She came in carrying a cardboard box of the sort one picks up at supermarkets. Grim-faced, she put it on Argand's desk and then stood back. Sweet lavender, soured perhaps by anxiety, fell again on the air and Argand sneezed.

He blew his nose. 'Well, Dm Madjen?'

'Yesterday evening, after you had gone to Catedratika Arendt's house, I cleared out Detective Ensign Focking's locker and desk. These are what he left behind.'

Argand stood, looked into the box. At first glance a miscellany much as you would expect: notebooks, standard issue, a heavy rubber-cased torch, a thermos flask. Petra Madjen dropped a long, white and very clean hand and lifted out a square black box of the sort one used to use for silver teaspoons. She dropped the catch and lifted the lid. Inside were a gilded chain, a silver cross with bars across each arm and an enamelled lapel pin of the same design.

'The insignia of the Chevaliers of Christ the Purifier. This interested me, Commissioner. The original Chevaliers were formed in the 1880s. My grandfather was one. Their object was to prevent East European Jews from settling in Brabt. And then I found this.'

A small black leather notebook, not official issue. On the first page Focking had drawn meticulously, childishly, the same barred cross. On the succeeding pages, one to each page, was listed every complaint the bureau had received up to the time of The Hok rally, the names and addresses of the complainants, a date, the nature of the complaint, and then, in red, a second date with a laconic 'beaten', 'threatened',

140

and so on. Finally, in green this time, almost every page ended with a final date and the one word 'withdrawn'.

For a moment, in a sort of psychic panic, the straight-jacketed, public-servant side of Argand's mind clung desperately to the hope that this was simply an *aide-mémoire* kept by a conscientious officer, but rationality prevailed and brought with it a wave of disgust and revulsion which almost made him drop the book.

The phone rang. The perfect secretary answered it.

'It's Detective Ensign Tremp. In Brichtzee. He says it's urgent.'

Argand took the phone. Tremp was breathless, excited, had two things to report and they came out muddled. In the end Argand, already flustered and confused himself, managed to sort it out. On one side, the State Security Police were objecting to Tremp's continued search through the Hotel Bristol, since a cache of tactical weapons was, they claimed, their business, no one else's. Under pressure Vustouk had delayed issuing further warrants and things were at a standstill. The other thing was this. That morning Vustouk's secretary had been seriously injured by a letter bomb and Vustouk himself hurt and badly shaken. And finally, Vustouk was asking most particularly and urgently to see Commissioner Argand. Would it be possible for Argand to drive over to Brichtzee, straightaway, and come to the old man's bedside?

Argand turned to Dm Madjen.

'At eleven o'clock you are to see a deputation of Turkish guest workers . . .'

Argand asked her to put them off. But politely. Make sincerest excuses. Yet secretly he was relieved. The law was so stacked against guest workers that he knew in advance he would be able to do little or nothing for them.

'Tell His Serenity that I will be in Brichtzee by midday at the latest.'

22

The bureau had been given a corner of the private carpark behind the Agricult Credit tower. There Argand surprised Bert Jenks, his driver, by getting in to the front seat beside him.

'Sergeant Jenks, I have something very important to say to you. Something you should give very serious attention to.'

Jenks sat motionless, gloved hands on the wheel. He was a stolid, heavy, sensible man, often with a glint of humour in his grey eyes, and occasionally, after lunch, the smell of schnapps on his breath. However, his driving was always exemplary.

'It's this. That accident when those gas cylinders came adrift was not an accident but an attempt on my life.'

Jenks did not move or speak, but a dimple that lay just behind the right corner of his heavy moustache deepened.

'It's not impossible,' Argand went on, 'that other attempts will follow. You must therefore be at risk. That's clear. Now, you are over the age of retirement, you are absolutely under no obligation . . .'

'Commissioner?'

'Yes?'

'Where are we going?'

'Well, I'm going to Brichtzee.'

'Then get in the back, where you belong, and we'll be off.'

It took Argand quite five minutes to recover from the not

unpleasant confusion this provoked: a sort of irritated anger not cancelled by but co-existing with an awareness that one was liked . . . But soon enough harder realities took over and, as they drove past Wilhelmspark and so into the industrial area round the docks, he considered again this terrible business of Focking.

He had brought with him Focking's notebook. Forty-eight red entries signifying intimidation. Thirty-two complaints withdrawn. The whole matter would have to be followed up, wherever it led, that was essential . . . His shoulders suddenly felt very tense, the back of his neck numb. It was all too much, he was being worked now as hard as ever before in his career. Really he should not be trying to find Focking's killer, it was wrong of Prinz to ask him to. Certainly much of the original motivation he had felt for the job had leaked away.

He looked sightlessly out over fields of stubble, some of which had been fired. A huge flock of seagulls signified that ploughing was already under way. Then, remembering, his head jerked round, checking the road behind.

A moment later Jenks caught his eye in the mirror. 'Don't worry, Commissioner. I've got my mind on it. I'll tell you the moment I'm suspicious.'

Argand smiled wearily, turned back to the notebook, the front page.

The Chevaliers of Christ the Purifier. State Trooper Kral had belonged to the same organisation. And somewhere else too he had heard of them, but where? Wearily Argand passed a hand over his face, then shook his head. Well, it would have to be followed through – with as much commitment, as much conviction, as the identification and arrest of Focking's murderer . . . of course, there might be a link.

Motive. Assuming Focking's killer to be the man who had cut down the flags, Argand had scarcely bothered to consider

143

motive. The man was about to be arrested, he had a knife in his hand, a swift, unconsidered thrust borne of fright. But now it seemed the killer was someone quite other after all. Of course it was possible he, or she (for a narrow, razor-sharp stiletto would require far less force than a heavy, broad sheath-knife), had killed Focking to protect the flag vandal. Though surely less likely. It would have been simple enough to obstruct Focking. But, if the killer had recognised Focking, knew Focking to be connected with the harassment meted out to complainants . . . well then! He leafed through the notebook again, trying to recall which cases Focking had been concerned with, who of the complainants had actually met him, would recognise him again. Without the records he could not be sure of all of them. But Paul and Mik Standen, certainly.

Vustouk's house was about the same age as its owner. It was a tall high-gabled building with long shuttered windows standing in a garden planted with exotic trees – a monkey puzzle, a douglas fir, a cedar. There was a gravel drive and forecourt, untidy with moss and weeds. Jenks parked the black Peugeot at the foot of a flight of six stone steps leading to a large heavy door fitted and studded with brass. Two Rural Guards flanked by small stone lions stood guard.

A servant, a young girl in black uniform, showed Argand through a gloomy hall cluttered with heavy polished furniture and up wide stairs. The landing was lined with books in uniform calf and locked up behind bronze grills. The smells were confused: leather, sandalwood, and old man. The latter was stronger when she opened a high door and announced him.

High pillows and a bolster propped up Vustouk in a massive bed. He was wearing a heavy flannel dressing gown over what looked like a nightshirt and on his head was what might have been a bandage, but was, Argand eventually decided, a small turban contrived out of a grey or off-white scarf.

The blind eye was swollen, protruding, white; the good one glittered beneath a bushy brow, then Vustouk found the eyeglass that nestled somewhere on the enormous expanse of his chest. He fitted it in.

'Commissioner. Good of you to come.' The voice rumbled from a phlegmatic chest, then, as it had in court, fluked up into an old man's treble. 'Sit, if you please, by the window. I can see you there. Yes. Good of you. You are busy, and I am a foolish old man.'

Argand settled himself in a large wooden chair, upholstered in cracked leather. This window was unshuttered, at the back of the house. More tall trees, dunes, a glint of sea.

'This is our sixth encounter, I think. But our first meeting.'

Argand assented with a nod.

'Three times I examined you as a witness. Once you were on my side. And twice before me, when I was a judge in the High Court. And I have followed your career. So you see, I know who I am dealing with.'

He sighed and the air seemed to rumble down cavernous galleries, then he stretched for a glass by his side. Argand handed it to him. Brandy and water. The hand that took it was fat and flaccid, chilly to touch and it shook a little.

'Serenity, I think perhaps I should not have come. Your health, injuries . . .'

'Poof. I was thrown over and I jarred my back. I was deaf for an hour.'

Argand perched on the edge of his chair waiting to take back the tumbler, but the hands held on to it firmly, resting it on the middle of Vustouk's large belly. The silence lengthened, and then the eyeglass dropped from the good eye and chimed on the rim. Still the old man did not move and Argand wondered if he had gone to sleep.

The rumbling sigh came again.

'In 1940 you were seventeen years old. At school. I believe you escaped to England.'

'In a fishing boat. Yes.'

'Then?'

'I had a cousin in the Brabanter air force who had flown his plane out. I got into contact with him and eventually I was given work as an apprentice aircraft artificer on the airfield where he and the other Brabanter pilots were based.'

'I stayed. I was already thirty years old, and a successful lawyer. So you see, Commissioner, I know what it was like.'

Argand presumed he meant the occupation. In fact the aircraft artificer had been parachuted back one month before D-Day to liaise with the Brabanter resistance, and had stayed underground in Brabt through the last six months. But he said nothing. He felt certain now that he was wasting his time, that he should look for a way of disentangling himself from what looked like being an embarrassing, time-consuming episode.

Vustouk drank off what was left; Argand stood this time for the tumbler, hoping to make the movement the start of his farewells. But the large clammy hand caught his wrist.

'Sit down, Commissioner.' The voice had authority this time – had quelled overreaching counsellors in court for twenty years or more. 'Kral, Commissioner. Kr-r-r-al.'

The name came off his tongue like an old lion's snarl.

'I was meticulous in that inquiry. I absolutely did not by one iota go beyond the very limited powers I had, not by even a hint of a suggestion. I thought that that way I would best serve your new bureau. Which I entirely approve.' A raised hand dismissed Argand's polite mutter. 'But that young

146

The turbanned head flopped back on the pillow; the eyeglass chimed again on the tumbler; one finger was lifted from it in what was, at last, and to Argand's relief, a gesture of dismissal.

Four hours later Jenks drove the large Peugeot surely but with just a touch of schnapped-up élan back to the City, and Argand mused darkly over a wasted and frustrating day. He had spent the end of the morning listening to the vapourisings of a senile old man. Admittedly Vustouk had had a very bad, a very nasty shock, but that did not render any more rational what he had to say – indeed, clearly the reverse. Released by Vustouk, he had decided to stay with Tremp and see the start of the gutting of the Hotel Bristol. But that had been held up by two State Troopers on the door, obsequious of course but firm, and finally aborted after three hours' delay by the Deputy Commissioner with a warrant issued over Vustouk's signature, authorising State Security alone to continue with the examination of the premises.

He scarcely noticed the fertile fens as they slipped by, petulantly ignored Jenks's cheerful acclamation of a windmill recently restored as a restaurant.

All that he was bringing back with him was the name again: Braun, this time Hans Braun. And that he would have learnt from Tremp's report anyway. Hans Braun instructing Lanning to hide the weapons. Gas cylinders crashing into a car travelling at eighty kilometres per hour. He shuddered, glanced past Jenks's head, then over his own shoulder.

A common enough name. There must be several thousand Brauns in Brabt, and perhaps hundreds called Hans. But he would have to be traced. And Jakob Braun was, just possibly, a lead. Odd, if they were connected, that he should be a Nazi enthusiast but Hans a communist of some sort.

Focking. He leaked the names of all who complained to the

bureau. But to whom? And who carries out the intimidation? This has to be worked on too. And already we are hopelessly overstretched. Can I spare men now to re-interview all those who dropped their complaints? Probably not. Not yet.

Argand looked despairingly out of the window. The road now swung round the first blocks of apartments on the outskirts of the City: on this side they were better constructed, better designed, better kept than on the road to The Hok. Here lived not guest workers in a ghetto but minor civil servants, senior clerks, people like Focking, and the better paid engineers, the highly organised dockers, and so on. Four traffic signs warning of crossroads, four of them in a row, had been altered with aerosol paint to look like swastikas.

For once Petra Madjen had gone home at a reasonable time. But she had left three notes for his attention. The first was from the quartermaster of the Mobile Operations Unit. It stated tersely that no losses of arms had been reported during the entire history of the brigade. A check of all armouries had, however, been authorised by the deputy commanding officer and would start early next week; a final result could not be expected until early in October.

Argand fumed – why could they not start immediately? It was absurd. The second note made him even more angry. It was from the same man, the MOBOP quartermaster, but timed three hours later than the first, and begged to inform the Commissioner that, since the Bureau of State Security was now handling the Hotel Bristol affair, the final report on the armouries would be sent not to him but to Commissioner General Gapp.

The third note was as bewildering, just as unexpected, but produced a quite irrationally cheering reaction.

Catedratika Julia Arendt earnestly requested Commissioner Argand to call again at her house, preferably as soon after eight o'clock as he could manage. She had something very important to tell him.

Before Argand left, he wrote a careful minute for Piet Stent, Commissioner for Crime, asking for an immediate Force Three interrogation of Jakob Braun, the particular thrust of the questioning to be directed at finding out if there was any connection between him and the Hans Braun of 2LM; even the possibility that Hans Braun had been the passenger in the Berliet truck should be examined. He felt a stab of shame as he did this – Force Three interrogation involves a measure of unpleasantness, and its use was something Argand normally deplored, only condoned when life was at risk, particularly that of uninvolved innocents. Well, what was known of Hans Braun was surely sufficient justification.

The minute was telexed to Crime, and then he left for an early supper at the Louis Bonaparte. There, over wiener schnitzel, he found his thoughts returning again and again to the frustrations of the day, the wasted journey to Brichtzee, the vapourings of Vustouk, culminating in the senile magistrate's refusal to give him a warrant to search the Hotel Bristol. Surely there was gross inconsistency there? But what could you expect from such an old man, unsupported by family or friends? I hope, Argand thought, someone puts me down before I drift into that sort of mental collapse. He shuddered, then drank up, conscious that for once his evening would be prolonged by pleasant company. And he wondered what Catedratika Arendt had in store for him.

23

The fact was, of course, that there had been nothing odd at all about Vustouk's decision to give State Security the warrant to search the hotel, and how it came about that that is what he did should be recorded.

Count Frederick, the Grand Duke's uncle, keeps a modest establishment in town: a small house not far from the Maria Teresa Palace near the centre of the City. It is built in the English style of Queen Anne, was erected for the Anglo-Irish mistress of the Grand Duke of that period. The interior has been restored to its original perfection, and by raiding the family's English properties the Count has managed to furnish it with Chippendale and Sheraton.

He likes the entertainment he offers, the small parties, the conversation and company to be correspondingly simple, elegant and unflamboyant. Consequently it was on pheasant pâté followed by truffle omelette served with one of the better Mosels that Baron de Merle, Chairman of EUREAC, Secretary Prinz and he lunched the day Argand visited Serenity Vustouk. Petits fours, coffee and a particularly pale armagnac remained on the table when he dismissed the servant and, as it were, brought the meeting to order.

'It's better sometimes if we can get together informally after a meal or whatever. Say what we like, not fret about the minutes or getting a quorum together.' He circumcised a cigar, graciously nodded acquiescence when Prinz lifted his pipe. De Merle polished gold-framed spectacles on his still-

new Secretary at the Ministry of Internal Affairs.'

The Count cleared his throat, his voice was mildly admonitory. 'Not really necessary, Baron, to say that sort of thing. You can be quite sure that both the Secretary and I put the interests of the state above personal considerations. You can also be quite sure that we are broadly in agreement with you as to what sort of government will best serve those interests.'

De Merle's head shuddered minutely, something between a tiny spasm and a voluntary shake.

'Very well then. What is to be done? What do we propose to do? You may remember that in June I suggested that we should avoid an election, should ally with the Protestants or the right. Prinz argued that such a coalition would last for only a limited period. I suggested that, during such a time, even if limited to only six months, we could use the resources of the state to destabilise Beck. As I remember, you voted down that proposal . . .'

'Are you suggesting we should reconsider it?' Prinz was as bland as ever.

'No . . .'

'I am glad.' The Secretary set down his pipe for a moment. 'It would not have worked then and it will not work now. The Protestants are, by and large, with Beck – because they don't like the nuclear plant at The Hok. And there are nine members of our party in the Moot who will not countenance a coalition with the right. Without them we cannot command a majority.'

He and the Count let the silence lengthen. Neither had any intention of helping de Merle come to his point.

The Baron threw back his armagnac as if it were schnapps.

'I do not think Beck should be allowed to hold this rally.'

'If we refuse permission, he will hold it anyway. Perhaps a few thousand less people will turn out. But there will be plenty.' Prinz sounded for once almost firm. 'And without permission they will be on the streets illegally. If that is the case, then the forces of public order will be duty bound to disperse them. It would be a bloodbath. And after the St Romain affair precisely not the sort of thing we want just now.'

'No. You misunderstand me.' De Merle's expression as he looked across the table at the still-urbane, even smiling public servant was baleful. 'Last week, at St Romain, Beck was not allowed to speak.'

The silence this time was indeed tense. For a moment neither the Count nor the Secretary could be heard or seen to breathe.

The Count: 'A vicious extreme left-wing group, recently snubbed by Beck, was the cause of the disturbance. I don't know the ins and outs of it all, but they called themselves . . .'

'No, sir.' Prinz lifted the stem of his pipe. 'I think what the Baron is getting at is this. The rally at St Romain was not broken up by the League of Marxist–Leninist Militants. It was broken up by the action of the State Security Troopers. Is that what you are drawing our attention to, Baron?'

'Yes.' De Merle spoke in a monotone now, keeping his voice unnaturally under control. 'I wish us all to understand the implications of that event. And to understand that at this stage I am talking only of implications. Nothing more. What was indicated to me by the intervention of the State Troopers at St Romain, what I have since had confirmed through clandestine channels, is that there are elements in the law-enforcement forces, and in State Security particularly, who, given the right sort of lead, are prepared to put the . . . er, facilities they have at the disposal of what at the moment I should call simply a "Stop Beck Movement". My sources have indicated that they are not alone. That there are other elements of a similar mind in the apparatus of the state. I

156

cannot help thinking that these, in conjunction with the Friends of Brabt and a substantial part of the industrial and financial sectors, could, in a situation which had been carefully prepared, ensure that Beck would not form a government.'

Count Frederick was an easy-going sort of person. A bachelor, a bon viveur who yet enjoyed his place near the centre of things in Brabt. It pleased him to chair the Grand Council, to hold a medieval sword at state occasions and to act as regent during his august nephew's very frequent absences. He got an even greater thrill out of the way in which the establishment of the PBDC had always courted him, sought his advice, admitted him to its inner councils. But at this moment he was suddenly gripped with icy apprehension. He foresaw a moment, perhaps imminent, when he would actually have to make a decision of consequence. Yet he was not a fool; his command of what had gone before, in spite of Mosel and brandy, was intelligent enough.

Absentmindedly he released an almond-paste comfit, shaped and coloured to resemble a tiny pear, from the brittle brown paper shell in which it had been nestling, and then dropped it, squashed, in the saucer of his coffee cup.

'You said, Beck should not be allowed to hold this rally.'

De Merle smiled at last. 'I should have said, "I do not think Beck will be allowed to hold this rally." '

'This seems . . . terribly rushed.'

'Not really. If it is done after he has announced, made a political reality of his alliance, it will be that much more difficult.'

'I am still not quite certain I understand . . .'

'And I would not dream of . . . compromising you by telling you. What I am trying to do is this. Having in some part heard of various meetings that have taken place; discreetly sounded out certain people; made my own estimate of

157

the situation; and evaluated the possibilities and likely outcome; I have arrived at a point where I think it advisable to prepare you, sir, as the most, um, positive member of our royal family, and you, Prinz, as the virtual head of our civil service and certainly of its most powerful sector, that there may be important roles for you to play in events that may shortly take place, and which could lead to the sort of outcome we all desire.'

Inwardly Prinz applauded this equivocation: crude perhaps, but you cannot expect exemplary finesse from people for whom it is not yet a habit.

'I think, Baron, you have made your point.' He beamed as broadly as he dared, but was feeling in his pocket for the lighter that would set his pipe going again. 'And I think that is as far as you should go at the moment.' Engulfed in Prinz's podgy fist, the gold engine flared and smoke settled round him again like a mantle. 'You have given us a great deal to think over. I think the least we . . . *I* can say is that you can, as I'm sure you are aware, be certain of . . . our deep sympathy for your predicament . . . which . . . as you have said . . . we to some extent share.'

De Merle looked down the table at the Count, who, perhaps a shade paler now, gave the briefest of nods.

'Very well. Very good.' He stood up, scraping his chair, and the Count touched a bell cord that hung against the wall. 'You have listened to me . . . with sympathy. That is a start. But there really is not much time, no time at all.'

The summoned servant handed him his sticks; he bobbed his head briskly at his host, blinked once at Wotan Prinz and allowed himself to be led away.

'More brandy?'
    'Thank you.'
    'This shouldn't happen. Should it?'

'Oh no. It's quite unthinkable.'

'Yet,' the Count replaced the stopper – it chimed delicately, 'we should not be too obviously in the ranks of those against them. De Merle and his friends.'

'No, indeed not.'

'You know, there are times when I rather wish my nephew was just a little . . . stronger-willed. Something of Juan Carlos, who is of course a second cousin, would be useful just now. But I think we should leave Wilhelm on his grouse moor, don't you? He'd only be in the way.'

This was close to *lèse-majesté*. Prinz merely nodded, though inwardly he agreed entirely.

They both sipped armagnac.

' "Other elements in the apparatus of the state." Who did he mean?'

'I rather think – sources have indicated – the Mobile Operations Unit.'

'Oh lord. Oh *Lord*. Perhaps we *should* get Wilhelm back. He is after all their Colonel-in-Chief.'

'No, no really. I do think better not. Count . . . um. Let me be a little open with you. What de Merle said this afternoon has not come as much of a surprise. It is a situation I have had my eye on for some time, and steps are being taken.'

'Situation in hand then, you'd say?'

Prinz frowned. 'I think so. But things have moved just a little more quickly than I anticipated. Nevertheless, yes, as far as this business of de Merle's is concerned, in hand.'

'And Beck?'

'Well – let's cross that bridge when we come to it. When all's said and done, Beck is politics, and as an Englishman I greatly admire once said . . .'

'A week in politics is a long time.'

The Count did Prinz the favour of taking him through the

marble hall to the door. He even stood in the portico and watched his stately progress to the corner of Wilhelmstras. A sound man, he thought. Very sound. Good record. Clever of course, but that may be just what we need at the moment. No, thought the Count with an accuracy Prinz would have found alarming, if we have anything to fear it's not his cleverness but a certain reluctance to act. He will leave things to the very last moment.

Very shortly after Prinz was back in his room in the Ministry, de Merle was on the phone to him.

'Secretary? There is a small thing you can do for us straightaway.'

'If it's in my power.'

'It is. Judge Vustouk at Brichtzee has asked you to decide whether he should authorise your new and, if I may so, rather absurd bureau to continue its examination of the Hotel Bristol or hand it over to State Security. It really is a matter for State Security, isn't it?'

This was undeniable on the face of it and therefore to deny it would be declaring opposition. Prinz allowed himself no more than five seconds and then assented. It would annoy Argand and that, in a sense, was a good thing. The more Argand felt disposed against State Security the more readily he would accept . . . well, whatever he would have to accept. Nevertheless, the poor man was working in the dark, and therefore slowly, and, as everyone seemed to have been saying all day, time was running out. Perhaps he should give Argand another nudge. Something in *Slik Stien* again? Or should he be more direct? He'd have to give it some thought.

24

The Dean-elect herself welcomed Argand on her doorstep shortly after eight o'clock. It had been a warm, sultry day but was ending well – the haze breaking up into cloud, higher cirrus above it catching the last warm colours, rose to gold, of a splendid sunset.

'Lovely, isn't it?'

Argand was not often asked to pass aesthetic judgements: he found himself at a loss.

'Yes. I suppose it is. I mean . . . of course. Of course it is.'

The small, dark but grizzled lady at his side lifted her head to indicate the park on the other side of the road.

'I hope you will come back in a month or so. The chestnuts are quite glorious then, especially in the evening.'

She led him not into the study where they had talked before but to a sitting room on the other side of the hall. It was furnished comfortably and well in a style not too distant from that of Argand's old flat, the one he had shared with his mentally deranged wife and precocious and pompous son until the latter had married and the former retired to Hearts Haven. The difference was that, where his furniture had been cumbersome, ugly and uncomfortable, hers was cumbersome, well proportioned and pleasant to use. Curtains and upholstery were equally pleasant to look at, though faded and in places worn – had Argand been interested in such things, he would have recognised Liberty prints three decades old.

Less easy on the eye was the man who now rose from one of the large square armchairs. He was of middling height, pear-shaped, had a large, ill-kempt blond moustache. His skin was brick-red and his nose was peeling. He was dressed in a loose-knit sweater that had holes at the elbows and the faded jeans he wore – most inappropriately for his figure – were grubby.

'Commissioner Argand, this is Licentiate Petersen of our Law Department.'

Petersen passed cigarette and tumbler of whisky into his left hand, expecting a handshake, but Argand had no more than a nod to spare before turning back to Arendt to assure her that he had eaten, that he wanted neither coffee nor drink.

'Good, good,' she cried, 'you are right. This is official, we must remain formal and businesslike.' She waved Argand into the other easy chair, perched herself on the arm of the sofa. 'So I shall be direct. Commissioner, when you were last here, you spoke of the League of Marxist–Leninist Militants, of the Hotel Bristol, and of their possible involvement in the murder of one of your men. We did, I think, mention that my colleague Licentiate Petersen was a member for a time, and it was he of course who initiated complaints against the police which resulted in the inquiry at Brichtzee. Well, after you had gone, I thought I should make myself useful and I tried to find Nik, Petersen that is, to see what he had to say about the League, and, well' – here she shrugged, spread her hands – 'no Nik. He had disappeared, almost without a trace, gone off in his camping-car to Yugoslavia.

'But now, as you see, he is back. And I have talked to him and he has talked to me, and I have convinced him he should talk to you.' She ended, head on one side, serious brown eyes fixed on the plump lawyer, who now twisted a little in his seat, lifted his glass, put it down, peered owlishly across the fireplace at Argand and then glanced away.

'Do you think I could have another drink, Julia?'

'No, Nik. Certainly not. You have had enough to raise your morale, another would compromise coherence. Begin please.'

'Where?'

'At the beginning, of course. Where else?'

The beginning was when Petersen had joined 2LM twelve months before, though its relevance was lost on Argand. Petersen had been asked to supply legal advice to a shop stewards' combine in EUREAC. He had been impressed with their militancy, their understanding of what he called their 'objective situation' and he asked to join. Once in, he had been invited to open a cell at the university, specifically to provide the League with cadres who would have the time and the expertise to organise the *agitprop* side of their activities; eventually it was hoped these would include publication of a weekly newspaper. By January things were going well and the exploratory talks had begun with Beck and the Reformed Socialists. Petersen had played a prominent part in these.

'Here I think you should admit,' Julia Arendt put in, 'that you hoped for a seat in the Moot yourself, is that not so?'

The red on Petersen's face deepened – with embarrassment or anger it was not possible to say – but he plunged on. One corner of Argand's mind registered the sureness of the Dean-elect's authority over a man he supposed to be awkward and dissentious: she really was an admirable woman.

In the spring things had begun to go wrong. First the EUREAC combine and then that at TULIP had pulled out: apparently both groups felt that with the steady move left of the Reformed Socialists – and Beck's constantly reiterated policy that the parliamentary party would actively encourage industrial militancy as an essential element in the progress towards a socialist state, there was no need for the League. Indeed, they felt their duty now lay within the Reformed Socialists, giving all the muscle they could to ensure there was no back-sliding on the part of the petty bourgeois elements who were still such a considerable force within the party. Ruefully Petersen admitted that they were probably right. Meanwhile, he was stuck with his university branch, by now the largest left. Having been the main force behind its creation, he felt reluctant to leave them in the lurch.

Again the Dean-elect interrupted, after first expressing irritation by flicking one sensibly shod toe to and fro. Ignoring Petersen, she looked straight at Argand.

'I do not suppose Nik will admit it to you. But the fact is he was by then emotionally infatuated with a really quite beautiful girl, a student in his department called Lisa Smit, who was secretary of the university branch. It was her idea that the whole branch should move to Brichtzee once the university closed for the summer and live there as a commune.'

'So . . . so what? It did not seem a bad way of spending the summer and, since I have a cousin who is a creditor of the firm that owns the Hotel Bristol, it was not difficult to organise the legal side of our occupation.'

Things had gone well at first, early July had been hot, the sea warm, it had been fun.

The raids by the Rural Guard came late in the month and Petersen had seen the chance here of reviving his political hopes by getting publicity through complaining to the new bureau. But in other ways they had a bad effect. Morale worsened, four or five people left, including two of the better-off students; it began to look as if they would have to close down before the end of the vacation.

Here Argand interrupted, 'Was the commune concerned with The Hok rally as early as this?'

'Yes. Three of us were on the committee of the Student Campaign Against Nukes, which itself had representatives on The Hok rally steering committee. So we were involved. But purely assisting with publicity, organisation, and so on. There was absolutely no one there who had any thought of disrupting it or creating a disturbance. Not at all. Not until those three turned up.'

His description of them matched Lanning the joiner's, and he knew their names. Besides Hans Braun, the two dark-haired brothers were called Mark and Seb Robart. They had money, acid and pot; after some discussion, a vote was taken and they were let in. Argand now opened his briefcase and produced a glossy blow-up of the best press picture of the flag vandal. Petersen unhesitatingly identified Mark Robart.

Argand shifted the picture so it no longer caught the light.

'Can you see any of the others here?'

Petersen bent over it, then shook his head. 'No. It's too blurred.'

Nineteen minutes to four on the town hall clock – that was clear enough behind the already severed Union Jack Robart was waving. It should mean something, Argand thought, but what? He rubbed his face in his palms – it would come to him later perhaps. Then he slipped the picture back into its envelope.

'You weren't there yourself?'

'No. And I'll tell you why not in a moment.'

The newcomers had kept very much to themselves. They took over a third-floor room, hardly ever went out, kept their clothes on, expected the others to bring them food, cigarettes, alcohol. Sometimes they were ill mannered, even bullying. They played cards. But most of the time they stayed put, and after a day or two it became possible simply to ignore them, pretend they weren't there.

Then, on their third or fourth night, a plain Renault van drove up to the door; the three men went down to meet it and carried up five heavy cases. The next day they asked the commune to find a joiner sympathetic to the movement. Lanning was already a regular visitor, had helped them get the place straight at the start of the summer . . .

'Didn't any of you speculate about those cases? Didn't you want to know why they needed a joiner?'

Petersen's eyes blinked, flinched away.

'Of course. And especially Wilhelm. Koonig that is. He was the only one of the . . . children I called them, who had actually done combat training on his state service.' This was likely enough: the rest, sons of professionals, technologists and so on, would have escaped the harsher brutalities of military life by one route or another. 'And he said the cases held weapons and that Lanning had hidden them. He said they must be terrorists, Red Spectre or some similar group . . .'

Koonig had pressed for a meeting to vote on whether or not the new arrivals should be allowed to stay but for one reason or another none of the rest had seemed eager to support him.

'What reasons?' Argand asked.

'Well, apathy in the first place. Things had got a bit slack by then. The children were bored, we had been there too long and, without the original political thrust of the League, there was no real motivation left. And, as I said, they had money and by then we needed it. And some of us, of them, were frightened. It was about this time Koonig met Braun on the stairs and took a nasty tumble, head-first. Braun was apologetic, and even Koonig agreed it was an accident, but, well . . .' Petersen shrugged.

Two days later the State Security raid took place. Koonig was beaten by Trooper Kral. Up on the third floor Braun received a bloody nose. But Lanning had done his job well and no weapons were found. However, the troopers did come across a map of The Hok plant which, they said, was classified material, and they took it away together with all the other stuff to do with the rally. Margarethe, Koonig's girl, said the map had been planted, probably by the Rural Guard during their previous raid. None of them had seen it before; it had turned up at the bottom of a cardboard box filled with duplicated handouts.

The third raid was really the last straw. Only Petersen's insistence that they should stick together to support his complaint of police brutality held them together, but Koonig's death really finished the commune. Within three days, only Petersen, Smit, Margarethe and the Gang of Three remained. Margarethe left the day after Vustouk's judgement – her parents were on holiday in Sardinia and they insisted that she join them there to get over Koonig.

Petersen and Lisa Smit stayed on for another week. The problem was that Petersen was afraid that, if he left, the terrorists would smash the place up and he would lose the deposit he had paid to the owners. Then, just about a week after the inquiry, Lisa went up to the third floor with food, entered without knocking and found the place strewn with weapons – they were checking them, Petersen supposed, cleaning, servicing them. What happened next was quite horrible. Lisa had no clothes on. The three men began to molest her, paw her about, and so on, and she screamed. Petersen heard, had the sense to get dressed, and rushed up the stairs.

'Well, when I saw the weapons – what looked like rocket launchers, machine-guns, bombs – I asked what the hell was going on.' Petersen's voice had sunk to a monotone, his chunky fingers twisted about between his knees. 'He, Braun, said they were to be used against The Hok plant during the rally. The bombs were to blow down the fences and, if they could get near enough, they were going to use the rockets on the reactor. They didn't expect to do any serious damage – but they'd certainly give everyone one hell of a fright . . .

'It was crazy, an absolutely mad scheme, and I told them so. I told them that right away I would expose them, that I was going straight down to the Rural Guard. And then they turned really nasty. Lisa was still there, sitting in a corner, crying. Well one of the brothers, Mark perhaps, kept me away from her, he hit me hard, a couple of times, and then kicked me. And the other two, well they went for Lisa . . .'

Arendt was sharp: 'Did they rape her?'

Petersen shook his head. 'Not . . . technically. But all but. They were very beastly. Braun . . . urinated over her. That sort of thing. And they beat me again, broke my glasses.' He gave a long shudder that spread out from his head and neck, his plump shoulders shook beneath the ragged pullover. 'In short, they scared us. Very thoroughly. Told us that, if we went to the police, then their friends, the ones who had brought the arms in the Renault van, would find us and we would be tried before a people's court and executed. I said I wouldn't go to the police, that if they let us go we'd get out of the Province for the rest of the summer, and Braun said that would be a good thing. We left for Yugoslavia that evening and we've been there ever since, until yesterday evening.' He took a deep breath. 'And what I want to know now is what steps you are going to take to make sure those thugs don't get at me or Lisa.'

He fixed a baleful eye on Argand, who met it straight but resisted the temptation to say that Petersen's attitude to the police appeared to be undergoing a change. Julia Arendt poured whisky for Petersen, Argand again refused.

'It's an odd business all the same,' she said, as she came back to the arm of the sofa. 'I mean, however much Beck has pulled the carpet out from under groups like the League, what these people told you they were planning seems . . . over-reaction, to say the least.'

Petersen looked over his glass. 'But that's just the point. They weren't League. They were Red Spectre. And they're against having any truck at all with bourgeois institutions or existing state apparatus. To people like that, Beck is the worst enemy of all, a reformist, a social democrat, a class traitor.'

'They would certainly have done him very great harm indeed if they had pulled off an attack on The Hok plant during the rally. Especially if it came out they were connected through the Hotel Bristol with the League. After all, up to the Wednesday before the rally, 2LM was still in name part of Beck's alliance.' Julia shook her head. 'It still feels wrong to me, quite wrong. Even Red Spectre depends for its existence on sympathisers almost all of whom, I imagine, like Beck. Destroying Beck would leave them isolated, cut off from support structure and supply lines.' She shook her head in doubt.

'But the attack was never made,' Petersen said. 'Perhaps they did think better of it, just for that sort of reason.'

Argand thought this over. 'No. I don't think that is what happened. It was the rain that stopped them. I imagine they planned to make their attack during Beck's speech. When that was rescheduled for the marketplace at St Romain, they improvised the flag incident instead.'

'Which ended in the murder of one of your men.'

Petersen shuddered again. 'If someone was killed and one of those three did it, my money would be on Braun. He's a monster.'

Argand silently agreed. And he thought too of the arms Petersen and Smit had seen, of how they remained unrecovered, and how very probably the monster had access to them.

25

Tremp smashed open the door with calculated suddenness. In the bright light of the precinct waiting room, Paul and Mik looked up – both pale and frightened, but Paul truculent too.

Tremp hooked a finger at Mik. 'Him. I'll take him first.'

He hustled Mik past the counter and into an interview room. As they went, the patron of the Aureole, leaning on the reception counter much as if it was one of his own bars, looked over his shoulder and called, 'Go easy on him, Officer. He's a good lad really.' Then he turned back to the duty officer, an old friend. They were reminiscing about the resistance. Remember old Whatsisname? How he found out that SS Oberleutnant used to smoke in the lavatory, and he managed to get the bowl filled with petrol, laugh . . . !

'Mind you,' said the duty officer, 'we were young then. Saw things too much as black and white. I'm not so sure which side I'd be on now. The National Socialists were right about some things, no doubt about that . . .' He paused, momentarily, and distantly a siren wailed.

Ambulances sped by through darkening streets, reminding bourgeois Brabt that doom at least is collective: one from the Bureau of Traffic Control headquarters, the other from Academikstras, where a yellow fire engine still stood by the smouldering wreck of a bombed black Peugeot. They met on the motorway box, sped on to Brabt state hospital.

Two stretchers slid from beneath raised hatchbacks and on to trolleys, rubber wheels whispered, a plasma bottle rang dully, large plastic doors that overlapped swung open and smacked shut, then the trolleys diverged – one to casualty, the other to the morgue. Policemen in traffic uniform – brown leather, bandoliers studded with reflectors – followed both, each to a point where they had to surrender the carcases, one still alive, the other definitely not, into the hands of medical science. Nothing left for them to do now but stand at a desk and assist the admission clerk with the form filling.

Braun, Jakob. Male. Age 38. Multiple injuries . . .

Name unknown. Male. Age unknown. Blown to bits . . .

'I should guess,' said the traffic policeman, the first to reach the wrecked Peugeot, 'an M26 fragmentation grenade was used. We've done a course to help us recognise that sort of thing, and that's what I'd say it was.'

'Well,' said the clerk, 'we'll know soon enough when the experts have done their bit.'

'You'll find I'm right.'

Mik would have done anything for Tremp, and if the policeman wanted him to talk then talk he would.

We were trying to get out. Get away. We'd only come for the music. And because of the rain there wasn't going to be any. So when that was certain we started pushing our way to the back, get a train back to Brabt, before everyone else there started doing the same. Well. We were just under the one with the English flag when that man went up it.

'No, it wasn't a lady helped him, but a man with long hair.

'And then I saw him. The policeman, Detective Focking, coming through the crowd – well, about five metres away when I first saw him, and at first I thought it was me he was coming for.

172

'Because . . .' (Because whenever anyone large and in authority has been coming, it has usually been me they were coming for: father with his leather belt; at school, Father Damien with *his* leather belt) . . . 'I don't know why because. I don't know.

'Of course we knew him. It was him came when Paul made the complaint. Detective Focking. He came to our rooms and asked us all about it . . . yes. Of course. I know it's about St Romain you want to know about.

'Well, the man up the flagpole came down and went on to the middle one and Detective Focking followed him. I don't think he even saw me, he was after the other man. He was shouting out how he was a policeman, how we should get out of his way and let him arrest the other man. Yes. Yes, he actually said something like "I am detective . . . yes, Detective *Ensign* Focking, I am going to arrest you."

'Well, then it happened. The stabbing, I mean. I didn't *see* the stabbing. The tall man, I think he did it, not the flagpole man. I didn't see the tall man had a knife. His back was to me.

'No. No. I told you. I didn't see the stabbing. But, you see, I recognised the man who cut down the flags. I'd seen him before. Yes. Quite sure.

'Well. That complaint I told you of. Well, after Paul made that complaint, and after Detective Ensign Focking had come to see us about it, these three men came to our rooms and, well, they really knocked us about quite a bit, and broke things and that, and one of them had this tattoo on his forearm – it showed just below his cuff, like a sort of scroll, and "Hath No Man" written on it. Yes. I'm sure. And the flagpole man had the . . .'

Unaware that a man sufficiently like him to be mistaken for him lay in pieces in the morgue at the other end of the hospital, Argand sat by Jakob Braun's bedside. Much of

Braun was bandaged or plastered. Apparently he had tried to break loose when being transferred from Traffic to Crime for questioning, had flung himself under a passing bus. Argand himself was swathed in surgical gown with mask, one mummy beside another, watching the slow fall of plasma above Braun's arm, listening to the shallow rasping breath of the man who had tried to kill him. Wires with sensors strapped to the man's skull and over his heart fed back impulses to a control room beyond a glass panel where a nurse knitted baby clothes. No need to watch the monitors too closely – they'd bleep if things took a turn for the worse.

The Commissioner shifted on the black PVC of the upright tubular chair. It was a long time since he had sat at the side of an unconscious man – he had forgotten how tediously time passes thus. Stent had rung him just as he arrived back in his apartment after walking from Julia-Arendt's house, had invited him to send one of his men over to the hospital, and Argand had chosen to go. For Stent had had more than Jakob Braun's accident to report. Braun's wife had now been questioned – there was a brother, half-brother or step-brother called Hans. And Hans had been at the campsite the night before the 'accident', had helped Jakob collect the cylinders and stack them on the Berliet, had left with Jakob that morning . . . Of course, Argand should have sent a subordinate, but his men were overstretched already – Tremp, for instance, was out questioning the homosexuals who had apparently been at St Romain and who had good reason to hate Focking; it was too important to leave to someone inexperienced. Thus Argand rationalised his decision. But much blacker doubts already moved like dark predators below the conscious surface of his mind.

Meanwhile, the tiny sounds and the more insistent smells of the place were getting to him – disinfectants, polish, the pepperiness of dry sterile cotton, not quite masking the presence of blood, urine, excrement. It was certain Jakob Braun would lose a kidney if he recovered; his colon was ruptured, the state of his liver and spleen remained uncertain. Argand's ears tuned to the tick of hot pipes changing temperature, the pulse of the electronic monitors, even, he fancied, the almost insect-like rattle of the nurse's needles on the other side of the darkened window. No, that could not be right – he could just see the wide, white wings of her headdress lit by the eerie glow from the monitors, but she was sealed away from him as efficiently as if he or Braun were radioactive. It must be some other part of the complex web of instruments and life-support systems that made a noise like the clacking of a beetle's wing-cases.

Strange that this man had tried to kill him; that, had that turning cylinder struck the windscreen of the Peugeot, it might well have been Argand on the bed strapped and wired to the devices that would not let him die. And stranger still that now, at this precise moment, the worthless Braun's life was probably worth more than Argand's, for on Braun's perhaps depended those whom his monstrous brother might kill in the future. Argand's skin again went cold as he thought of the madman aiming heat-guided missiles at the nuclear reactors . . . He leant a little nearer Jakob Braun, tried to detect any change in the dying man's breath, in the pallor of the shredded skin beneath bright orange mercurochrome. And so he missed the visitor who had slipped noiselessly into the intensive-care control room, was unaware that the nurse had stopped knitting . . .

'And the flagpole man had the some tattoo . . .' Smack. Tremp hit Mik, open-handed but hard, across his cheek and ear.

Mik howled. Then: 'But it's true, I swear it, and gold crowns on his teeth at the back . . .' Smack.

Tremp, his hand stinging, sat back and looked at the now whimpering wreck in front of him. Like his chief, Tremp was near the end of his tether. For several weeks he had been doing entirely alien work, hunting down his own colleagues, trying to get them suspended, reprimanded, pilloried in the media. There had been few satisfactions – really only the inquiry at Brichtzee, where it was quite clear that State Security Trooper Kral was a thoroughly nasty piece of work. Since then the job had got sourer, the only relief being the work he had done on the Focking case.

'Now tell the truth.'

Mik sobbed for breath. 'But I am. They beat us up, broke up all our things, and one of them had this tattoo, the scroll. "Hath No Man", it said.'

'And you're saying that same man, with the same tattoo, was the man who cut down the flag of Brabt at St Romain.'

'Yes.'

Tremp held himself back for twenty seconds. His eye glanced over the reddened, tear-stained face in front of him, the shoulder-length dark hair tousled up like a woman's. He smelt urine and his lip curled. The nasty little faggot has wet himself. The skin crept on his buttocks, his scrotum tightened. Mik, he thought, is not only a queer, he's probably a Jew too, and he hit him again, six times, relished the sudden splash of blood on the edge of his hand, the smear across Mik's cheek. He pulled out a handkerchief, pushed it into Mik's hand and waited until the blubbering had subsided.

'Now then. I want you to remember that. Remember that that's the sort of thing we hand out to malicious liars. And I'm warning you. If you repeat that story, there may be a comeback. Lies told to a policeman in the course of his duty are an offence.'

'I . . . told . . . no lies. No. Please. Not intentionally. It's what I thought I saw, honestly it's what I thought I saw.'

Calmer now, Tremp looked Mik over again. A sorry specimen. No backbone at all. Not a likely sort to try deliberately to slander the armed forces. Probably, thought Tremp, he's been put up to it.

Jakob Braun's head jerked spasmodically three times, his last breath caught on a blob of phlegm in his upper trachea and its dry rasp became a rattle. Argand, horrified, stood and for one moment thought that the masked, gowned figure on the other side of the glass was his own reflection, but then it turned. Argand reached the darkened corridor just as the plastic doors at the far end slapped shut, black then silver in the light, then black again. He hurled himself towards them, felt his leather-shod feet lose purchase on the vinyl floor, crashed through the doors and saw on the landing that one of three lifts was sinking to the ground floor where the other two already were.

Back in the unit, two of the monitors bleeped frenetically and lights flashed. The third was dead. The nurse bled from where her fall had driven one of her own knitting needles into her side. Argand checked that the wound was minor, that, although unconscious from the blow that had struck her down from behind, she seemed at least to be alive. Not so Braun. The leads which ran from the sensors fastened over his heart had been pulled apart at a jack and socket connection, and the jacks had then been pushed into a two-socket power point. Enough to snuff out what little life had still flickered in the abused and broken frame.

26

With Jakob, the best possible lead to Hans had gone. Neither State Security nor Crime had anyone on their files who would fit; none of the known members of Red Spectre looked like him. The only traceable relative was Jakob's wife – but she hardly knew Hans, she said. He came on visits about once a month and when he came she kept herself and the two small children out of the way. No doubt Crime working with the Rural Guard would soon piece together the earlier history of the family, but there was no reason to believe that would bring them any nearer the actual whereabouts of Hans. And he was a killer, armed with sophisticated and vicious weapons, yet ready to improvise with gas cylinders, electrically charged wires, ready to kill spontaneously, on impulse.

Argand sat at his desk, shoulders hunched, head drawn in like a sullen, day-dazed owl, and went over again as much of all the heterogeneous information he could recall about the League of Marxist–Leninist Militants and the Hotel Bristol. The trouble was that he no longer had the documentation: it had gone to the State Prosecutor's office where someone was taking far too long over deciding whether or not Kral should be charged with culpable homicide.

They told him that the lawyers would be through with the papers in five or six days' time and that it would not be in order for the Commissioner to come over now . . . the feeling that everywhere doors were shut to him, obstructions placed

178

in his path, almost that a gladiatorial net had been cast over him, became very real. Argand reached for the tranquillisers he now hardly ever took, rejected them, phoned Secretary Prinz instead. Miraculously – as when a jammed door gives unexpectedly – the position was reversed. Within an hour the entire file would be available, would he like to send someone for it?

Meanwhile, he again looked over the official report on the bombed Peugeot. The weapon had certainly been an M26 grenade, the coiled inner lining of which bursts into hundreds of razor-sharp fragments – these had shredded the interior of the car, including its occupants.

The passenger had been a Belgian ear, nose and throat specialist who had been attending a seminar at the Brabt Medical Faculty. He had been on his way back to Brussels when his car pulled up at the controlled crossing in Academikstras opposite the Engineering Faculty. A preliminary check with Belgian Security had revealed no likely motive for the attack and it was being provisionally assumed that the car had been bombed in error.

Had I not walked to Catedratika Arendt's house, I should have passed that way, thought Argand, and in a chauffeur-driven black Peugeot. It is surely not paranoia to surmise, if not suppose, that I was the intended victim. But if I was, then someone somewhere tipped off the killer that I was in the vicinity . . . Petersen? The Catedratika herself? A cold sickness blossomed out from the pit of his stomach as the logic of the situation pushed him on, but it could not hinder its progress. No one else whose political views were even remotely towards the end of the spectrum occupied by 2LM had known where he was. But it was, was it not, possible that the information might have been passed on innocently?

Before he could pursue this further, the Hotel Bristol papers arrived, and he called Tremp in to assist him. There were a lot of them: the initiating sworn complaints, depositions, subpoenas, a transcript of the inquiry, and so on, and also all the papers the State Security Troopers had themselves taken from the hotel – three reams of duplicated handouts against nuclear technology, several thousand more advertising the rally, paperbacks on the subject, and so on.

Argand recalled how Petersen had said that Margarethe, Koonig's girlfriend, asserted that a map of The Hok had been planted on Koonig, then how Hans Braun had told Petersen that they intended to use the grenades to get through the perimeter and so into rocket range of the reactor. This plan surely depended on having a map.

It was not a connection, more a repetition, but with nothing else to go on Argand suggested they should concentrate on finding it.

They searched for ten minutes or so, then Tremp turned it up.

An A4 sheet of photocopy paper, a map on one side – a good copy, from a good-quality machine – a map, clearly, of The Hok plant. In the bottom right-hand corner a rectangle had been blocked out – presumably pasted over on the original. It was fair to suppose the blocked-out section indicated where the map had come from. Whoever had made the copy had wanted to keep that a secret.

Argand thought aloud: 'You can tell a lot from a map, you know.'

'Yes, Chief. Where you are and where to go.'

'Of course. But in a place like The Hok you know where you are, and once you're there there *is* nowhere to go.'

'I wouldn't say that, Chief. Complex place. And some areas dangerous. I'd like a map if I was put down there.'

'All right. But this one wouldn't help much. It's on too small a scale to show that sort of detail in the plant itself. Just the main features. But there's a lot of detail of the land around, and even the sea and river.'

'So what else could it be for?'

'Let's work that out. Lots of people have special maps. Electricity suppliers, water suppliers, that sort of thing. Even a birdwatcher could want to make a detailed map of The Hok. But if he did, it would look very different from this. What do you make of it?'

'Well. It shows the perimeter fences in detail and the watchtowers. The contours are clear and even variations in vegetation . . . honestly, Chief, it's what I'd expect, a map modified to serve as a base on which to work out a plan of attack.'

'But you're wrong, you see. I worked on the plan for the new Arts Faculty and I advised on the American military base on Santa Caridad – both from the point of view of internal security, and in the latter case thinking of small-scale commando attack as well. Well, now look at this. These dotted lines indicate interior lines of communication for bringing troops quickly but under cover to trouble-spots. This line of crosses shows the second line of defence if the force has to withdraw from its first position, and these show firepoints from which their retreat will be covered. And then do you see what these are, more dotted lines running just below the low-tide mark? They must be an early-warning system against attack from the sea. Don't you see what I'm getting at? This is a military map, yes, but one prepared by people more concerned with defence than attack.'

Argand straightened, palms pressing in the small of his back. His eyes glowed with excitement as his mind ranged like an electronic scanning device over the previous weeks, picking out a score of apparently unrelated details, questions, doubts, trying each in turn against the hypothesis that had blossomed in his brain, full grown, completely developed, as all the best ideas are. They all fitted.

'The Mobile Operations Unit is responsible for the defence of all nuclear installations,' he began. 'Your joiner Lanning identified the MOBOP stencil although it had been . . .'

'Jesus Christ.' Tremp had gone white, and grey triangular smudges beneath his eyes suddenly gave his rather plump face a clownish look.

'What is it?'

'Last night. That . . . pervert. I didn't believe him. He said the man who climbed the flagpole had a tattoo on his forearm. He couldn't see all of it. Just . . . "Hath No Man".'

Argand nodded furiously; excitement now seemed most untypically to consume him. 'Just so, just so. *Greater Love Hath No Man*. The MOBOP motto.'

'It can't be possible.'

'It is possible. These days it is possible. Why, there are elements in the army who even want to form a soldiers' trade union. And it explains so much. Some left faction, Red Spectre perhaps, names don't matter, has somehow contrived to infiltrate the Mobile Operations Unit. And Lord knows what else . . .'

Twenty minutes later Prinz came bustling down the stairs into Argand's office, smoke pumping behind him, face beaming, handshake warm but brisk. Tremp collected himself sufficiently to whisk a chair beneath the large bottom, and then, to his chagrin, was dismissed.

'Right, Jan, let's have it.'

But the broad rosy features of the Secretary quickly clouded as Argand produced and substantiated his hypothesis. He fidgeted, looked glum, stuck out his moist bottom lip. Argand grew irritated, aware of the reception he was getting, cast about for supportive indications that had not yet occurred to him, outlined the sort of checks the military should make, what action he would take if he were in their place. And Prinz's face grew . . . not longer, his face could never be a long face, but darker, gloomier.

At last Argand could think of no more to say. Prinz hoisted himself to his feet, took a slow turn round the room, paused, thumbed tobacco into his pipe and lit it.

'Fascinating, Jan. Quite fascinating. I've listened to you with the very greatest interest, I assure you.' He breathed out a long sigh, turned again, looked up through the window at the feet and legs of the customers of Agricult Credit. 'But you know it is all so circumstantial, so speculative. Look. Let me put this to you. Everything you have said, every demonstration you have produced, would work just as well if the boot were on the other foot.'

'Secretary, I don't at all follow . . .'

'No, Jan, listen. You have produced a model, an hypothesis. The Mobile Operations Unit has been infiltrated by left-wing terrorists. And you find that, applying this model to a wide-ranging set of diverse data, it works. But that's not enough. As I said. Suppose it was like this: elements of the Mobile Operations Unit have infiltrated a left-wing group – then couldn't everything you have adduced to support your hypothesis be applied to support its opposite? I think that might be the case.' He took another turn. 'I know what I have just said is utterly absurd, and, yes, Jan, I do think you are on to something. I really do. But before I spring your idea on the Secretary of Defence I'd like you to spin it around a bit more, think it over. Do as I suggest. Stand it on its head. I mean, I do think you have to apply that test – it would be too silly to have it all thrown back at us that we'd caught quite the wrong end of the stick . . .'

27

Six hours later, well after night had fallen, Argand returned home. He felt confused and dispirited and, when he entered the foyer of his apartment block and a tall lady, fiftyish, very expensively dressed in black silks and diamonds, a cashmere cardigan over her shoulders, rose from the leather and stainless-steel bench and came towards him, hand out-stretched, his bewilderment was complete.

'Commissioner Argand. I'm so pleased I've found you.'

She had heavy thick hair, silvered and streaked, and dark eyes that seemed luminous. Her beringed fingers were thin and perfectly manicured, and only a puffiness beneath her chin and the scarcely perceivable presence of very expensive corseting suggested that she was not quite as well preserved as she might wish people to think.

'Sarah Frankel,' she said. He touched her hand as briefly as politeness allowed.

The name took a second or two to register, then: 'Dm Frankel, I take it you want to see me on a matter concerning the bureau. You should call there, perhaps first arranging an appointment by telephone.'

Her eyes glowed and she shook her head as if burdened with some undefinable sorrow.

'But that is precisely what I cannot do. What, Commis-sioner, I am frightened to do.'

Argand was brusque. 'There is nothing to fear, I assure you . . .' With Focking dead, this seemed, on the face of it, to be true. 'Now, I have had a busy day and I advise you to ring the bureau in the morning.'

She seemed not to be listening, was delving into a large black leather purse. From it she produced a piece of expensive paper, folded twice.

'Please read this. Not the whole thing, just what it says at the bottom.'

Argand did not need to read the main part. It was another copy of the Reverend Merck's letter introducing the material advertising the Friends of Brabt and the Festival of Moral Regeneration. The only difference between this and the one Petra Madjen had put on his desk three weeks ago was that a typewritten postscript had been added. This invited Dm Frankel to contribute the sum of fifty thousand gelds. If she did not, her face would be slashed in such a way as to mark her for life – like *this*. And here a pencil had scrawled a Star of David. She watched his eyes, observed a reaction, and added, 'This is not the only thing of its kind that has happened.'

Argand handed it back. 'You had better come up,' he said.

In the lift he felt profoundly uncomfortable. She stood firmly in the centre. She smelled of the sort of perfume his peasant mother had told him was worn only by whores. When they left, her skirts rustled . . .

She went straight to his window and exclaimed at the view, the lights of the City, the sweep of the river marked by its bridges, the presence of the darkened fens beyond. It was as good or better, she asserted, than that from her house on the hill behind Wilhelmspark.

'We are quite near the top, you know. Only the Prinzes' house is above us, Wotan Prinz that is, the Secretary . . .'

But Argand's mind was too near to being overthrown to mark this. Desperately he sought stability of some sort.

'Recently I have formed the habit of having lemon tea

when I get home,' was the best he could manage.

'I should love some.'

Relieved to be in his small kitchen, he wondered if he had any biscuits he could offer her, anything to push back the implications of what she had already revealed, push them back until he had the whole story from her.

Seated at his table, he invited her to tell him everything else there was to tell. She shrugged back her cardigan and diamonds flashed, indicating discreetly the half-inch of cleavage thus exposed.

'It started, of course, after I had complained to your bureau about the traffic policeman who called me a fat Jewess. The day after he was suspended, for a week only on full pay, a pig's head was thrown over our garden wall. There was a paper pushed through a hole in one of its ears. My husband threw the paper away, but I can remember every word.'

'Go on.'

'It said fat Jews should be treated as this pig had been treated, and if we went to the police or back to your bureau they would know, and something like this, like the pig, would happen to us. We did nothing, heard nothing more for several weeks. But now this.' She tapped the purse again. 'It came three days ago and it has taken me this long to make up my mind about what to do about it. But this morning I received an obscene telephone call, the point of which was to ask why I had not yet paid up.'

'Your husband knows?'

'No. I have so far been able to keep it from him. He leaves quite early in the morning for his office in Randstras . . .'

Argand nodded. Randstras was the centre of the Brabt gem market, second only to Amsterdam.

'. . . and he is worried, so worried. If he knows it still goes on, he will insist we go back to New York. We met there as children in the war. Both families went there in 1939. And came back again. Not many of us came back.'

Again Argand nodded, this time impatiently. He knew why few of the exiles had returned. The collaborating government of Brabt had not been at all reluctant to help the Gestapo round up non-Aryans. At the occupation there had still been fifteen thousand Jews in Brabt, nearly all in the City. Nine hundred survived.

He questioned her carefully, concealing the desperation he felt, about all the circumstances surrounding the three threats, but found out nothing further. He advised her to send a cheque straightaway – apart from the risk she ran by not doing so, later investigation to find out who handled it at the Friends' headquarters, who knew of its arrival and so on, would provide useful leads. He promised her that he would do everything he could to maintain secrecy, that he would tell no one at all that she had called until he had worked out a safe way of dealing with it all. She accepted all this and undertook to phone him at home if there were any more incidents.

At last she stood up to go, pulling her fine cardigan back around her shoulders, and he almost hustled her out on to the landing, barely allowing her jewelled fingers to touch his. As the lift door closed, he bolted back to his rooms. For an hour or so he paced back and forth, occasionally pausing at his large desk – it had been his father's and was the only piece of old furniture he had retained – to jot down each link, each piece as they fell into place. None of this was comfortable nor comforting, but at last he felt he had it right.

It was near enough midnight when he stopped. He slumped into an armchair and sat there, brooding over the city from his darkened eyrie. 'What is sanity?' he had once asked Dr Liszt. And the answer had been: 'The ability to recognise the real. Not an easy matter when the real runs counter to all one's most deep-rooted, unconsidered, even unconscious beliefs and presuppositions.'

No, it had not been easy. It had been painful. Not only that; the sanity that had resulted was an uncomfortable business. Another of Dr Liszt's dicta was thus also substantiated. Answering Argand's concern for his wife, the good doctor had said, 'Sanity is not happiness. The insane are often happier than the sane – that is why they choose to be mad. And indeed why so many of us are.'

So Argand was not happy, though he recognised a grim satisfaction coupled with a special sort of anxiety not unlike that experienced by artists when they know they have it right in their heads but fear the execution will fall short. He knew the days ahead would be difficult, as difficult as any he had known. Difficult and dangerous.

He reproached himself too. After all, neither Prinz nor Sarah Frankel had said as much as Serenity Vustouk. To his chagrin he now found, on top of everything else, that his self-respect was dented by the fact that he had dismissed the magistrate's warnings as the vapourisings of a half-blind, senile old man. Still, there was no point, nothing to be gained from self-recrimination. He stood up and returned to the monstrous desk. For a second he looked sightlessly into the eyes of his father whose framed photograph stood on the top, then, late though it was, tore off the top sheets of notes he had already made and began meticulously to plan what should be done.

PART FOUR: CONCLUSIONS

28

During the next twenty-four hours his presence, for the most part a disembodied voice on the telephone, moved discreetly through the corridors of power. Dm Madjen was instructed to say to callers at the bureau that he was back in St Romain on business connected with the murder of Focking. In fact not even she knew where he really was. By two o'clock in the afternoon he felt confident that things were going as they should and he reappeared in the basement of the Agricult Credit tower, where he had an appointment he felt he should keep. He did not take a bus and then walk; instead, the bullet- and rocket-proof car with motor-bicycle escort (usually reserved for the less popular visiting heads of state) that Prinz now insisted he should use moved about the City by devious routes.

His successor at the Bureau of Public Order arrived about ten minutes behind him by more conventional means.

Pranck was a tall gangling man with thin limbs, large hands and feet, a large beak-shaped nose and no chin to speak of. In the past, as Argand's deputy, he had been faultlessly efficient, entirely without imagination and incapable of making a decision on any question that was not purely technical.

'This rally on Saturday,' he began. 'The Reformed Social-ists and their allies. Beck speaking in Wilhelmspark. Well, Commissioner General Gapp has some crazy notion about it that has quite floored me. I hope you don't mind if I ask your opinion of it.'

Argand signalled his readiness to listen.

'It's quite simple really. He wants to deploy the entire uniformed section of his State Troopers, call in a thousand Rural Guards and put the Mobile Operations Unit on alert. And I don't see why. There's no need, no need at all. It's to be a simple straightforward march from the university to the park, we've had no dispute with the organisers over the route, or anything like that. There really doesn't seem any reason at all why Public Order and Traffic shouldn't handle it in a purely routine way. What do you think I should say to him?'

'Have you spoken to Secretary Prinz?'

'Yes. He told me to see you. Said he was very busy with something else.'

For once that could just be true, Argand thought. All the same, he should not have ducked.

'He said your advice would be good enough – that, if you think Public Order and Traffic are sufficient, then they would be, and I should oppose Gapp's suggestion.'

Argand thought this over. The hint was clear enough. With the picture that was beginning to emerge, the last thing that was wanted was that the entire operational elements of State Security and MOBOP should be on standby in the City. He made a show of going over the route with Pranck, of checking the estimated numbers who would march and attend the rally. Finally he said, very firmly, that no troops would be needed, there was no way he could see that the security of the state was threatened, the rally was entirely constitutional, organised by one of the parties in the ruling coalition, and so on. At the very most, Pranck might ask Commissioner Wynand for two hundred Rural Guards to be held in reserve, perhaps in the Luna Park just down river from Wilhelmspark – that would be ample.

Pranck was effusive – something Argand never enjoyed.

'I really am grateful. You've no idea how supportive I find it that I can turn to you . . . I mean, many people in your position would be happy to leave me to flounder on my own.'

At five o'clock Prinz rang.

'Jan, you gave Pranck the right answer. I hope you didn't mind my passing him on, but I thought it best for him to make his own decision rather than hide behind my authority. But I'm afraid Gapp isn't taking it well. As soon as Pranck passed on your joint decision, he called another emergency meeting of the Committee of Public Safety to press to have it overturned. Now I think I have worked out what to do about this, and I'd like you to come over to the Ministry to discuss it. Yes. In the state sardine can. I will not have you walking.'

29

At the end of the day one last element had to be fitted in. Argand arrived at the Louis Bonaparte at about nine in the evening, by which time most solid bourgeois Brabanters have eaten and gone home. The manager was not surprised – the Honest Commissioner had been known to dine, almost always on Wiener Schnitzel with a glass of Mosel, as late or even later. But never before had he asked for one of the three private rooms the Louis Bonaparte still maintained on the first floor – charming relics from the 1880s when the restaurant had been opened.

Gossiping with the head waiter, the manager guessed that some senior government official would join Argand, or an industrialist or financier keen on recruiting a highly respected police officer, not above two years off retirement, to his board. The head waiter, not out of conviction but because he knew it was expected of him, took the more traditional view. Ten years had passed since they had seen Argand's wife there – they were about to be privileged to see her successor.

Twenty minutes later the head waiter claimed the bet they had struck, for a lady indeed did arrive, and exactly the sort of lady the staff of the Louis Bonaparte most admire. In her early fifties she wore a light fox fur, her silvered hair was meticulously dressed, a simple number in black lace set off to perfection both embonpoint and diamonds. Her perfume could not have retailed at less than ten thousand gelds for a hundred grams. And while she certainly had her figure under control it was by no means underfed.

'A divorcée,' suggested the wine waiter.

The head waiter was more gallant. 'A widow,' he asserted, and kissed the air. 'No one in their right mind would divorce such a woman.'

She stayed with Argand for only forty minutes and, to the entire establishment's dismay, had nothing but pretzels and Perrier while the Commissioner seemed satisfied with decaffeinated coffee. The Louis Bonaparte's collective disappointment was complete when she left in a taxi a full quarter of an hour before Argand. The waiter who later cleared up the private room, oak-panelled with discreetly erotic carvings and a good copy of a Boucher, declared that the cushions on the couch were quite undisturbed and that the only hint of vice to be found was an ashtray filled with cigarette stubs. At least they were gold-tipped.

The next day Dm Sarah Frankel, wife of Amos Frankel the diamond merchant, laid a formal but unpublicised complaint, not with the Bureau of Advice and Investigation but with the fraud branch of the Crime Bureau, against the Friends of Brabt and the Festival of Moral Regeneration. She claimed extortion and forgery: first that a cheque had been extorted from her, which was true; secondly that the cheque had been increased by a factor of ten before being cashed, which was not true but was thought to be a necessary exaggeration if the appropriate warrants were to be obtained. They were, but still the organisers moved behind elaborate smokescreens and it was generally supposed that the target of the raid was to be the finance section of the Dockers' Union.

Officially, Argand played no part in this. He spent the next two days in his office coping with an irate deputation of

Turks who had returned from their annual break in their homeland to find that their jobs at EUREAC had disappeared. Even Dm Madjen was surprised at the single-minded commitment he brought to the hopeless task of getting their case the fair hearing he knew they deserved. She was surprised, and dissembled her disapproval.

30

'According to our constitution, an extraordinary meeting to discuss one matter of vital interest to the safety of the state can be called if two of our members are agreed that a situation has arisen that warrants it. Excellency Argand, Commissioner of the Bureau of Advice and Investigation, has called this meeting, and he is seconded by Excellency Stent, Commissioner for the Prevention and Detection of Crime. I shall ask each to speak in turn before the rest of us and I now call upon Excellency Argand to open.'

For a moment not even the sound of an indrawn breath broke the silence. Then Secretary Prinz's gold lighter grated and flared and the spell was broken. One Excellency let out a sort of hoot, another banged the table in front of him, a third swore. Only Argand and Stent, a large florid man, and of course Prinz himself remained outwardly unmoved, though the knuckles on Argand's hand whitened as the pressure of his fingers on his pen increased.

Gapp's voice was a savage yelp: 'Point of order.'

Prinz beamed through smoke. 'The Chair recognises Excellency General Gapp, Commissioner for State Security. And would be inclined more favourably towards him if he recognised the Chair.'

'Chairman, Excellencies, I am raising a point of order.'

'Pray continue.'

'I thought this meeting had been called at my request, to discuss a proposal in which I am seconded by Excellency

Wynand of the Rural Guard.'

'It is,' said Prinz, in his most agreeable tones, 'an unusual situation. Two days ago I received two requests that we should meet today. However, the statutes under which we exist have made provision for such an occurrence.' He opened a thin leatherbound book which lay on the table in front of him, and a podgy finger tracked along the line. ' "The Chairman, or Secretary for Internal Affairs if he happen not to be Chairman, shall place that proposal first which he deems most to bear upon the security of the state . . ." An awkward position to be in, especially since I have heard only simple statements unbacked by argument. However, the statutes have been prepared with just such an indecisive old buffer as I am in mind . . .' This was a joke: ten years earlier he had drawn them up himself. No one laughed. ' "All other things being equal," it goes on to say, "that proposal which was received first will be heard first." I think that answers your point of order. Proceed, Excellency Argand.'

Gapp snapped back, 'May I ask Argand at what time precisely he lodged his proposal at your office.'

Prinz closed the leather book, took off his bifocals. For a moment his watery blue eyes remained fixed on General Gapp, then he said quietly, but with more strength in his voice than any of them there had heard before, 'You may not.'

Gapp sat back. A mottled hand passed over his silvery blond hair, then fingers tapped a hard staccato on the polished surface in front of him. 'This is a charade,' he muttered.

Argand patted the thin pile of double-spaced typed A4 in front of him so the edges were exactly neat, cleared his throat, looked round, received a nod from Prinz, and so began.

* * *

'Chairman, Excellencies. I intend first to present you with a large collection of facts, of evidence; then I will offer an interpretation of them; and finally I shall ask you to endorse my proposals concerning them.

'You all know what my bureau has been doing for the last ten weeks. It has twice been discussed by this committee. It has not been pleasant work. Disagreeable because you are my colleagues, and your men are the colleagues of my small team. But it has also been . . . unpleasant to discover that a very high proportion of the complaints made were justified.

'In many cases this turned out to be because our laws and guides for our conduct as policemen were made for other times, a different society – they simply will not work under present conditions. Only in the area of terrorism have these things been brought up to date. But this is an exception. In most areas police action is over-restrained in ways most inappropriate to this day and age.

'So. Many of the complaints that reached my bureau were justified, but only by the letter of outmoded laws, and under protest I had to record them as justified and take appropriate action. But it grieved me to find that many too were justified by any standard of decent, civilised behaviour you may care to work by. Far too many. To begin with, this merely troubled me, though I did not then see the pattern behind it all which I think is now evident.

'Here are some examples. A lady of irreproachable respectability is gratuitously insulted by a traffic policeman. A youth is beaten by precinct officers because he is thought to be a homosexual. I know we all detest sexual perversion in any form . . .' (Prinz's gaze flitted to the small chandelier above the table, but his entirely serious expression did not alter by a micron) . . . 'I am sure we also detest much more illegal, purposeless, vindictive violence, especially when it is our men who carry it out.

'Let me go on. A trade unionist, a docker, is beaten on an entirely peaceful and legal picket line. He was protesting at the export of arms to a government of which he disapproves, as, in a limited and prescribed way, he is entitled to do.

'Then there is another area I should like to draw your attention to, that of guest workers. One case in particular came to my attention only a few days ago. It involved Turkish construction workers employed by EUREAC at the new Spartshaven plant. Seventy of them returned from their holidays to find they had been dismissed *in absentia*, and thereby the rights guaranteed to them under EEC rules had been circumvented. The outcome was that they, and several had their families too, were herded on to an old fourth-class railway carriage which, after five days, will arrive back in their country. The Rural Guard in whose jurisdiction they had lived did this, empowered, I admit, by a magistrate's warrant that allowed them to use "whatever force they deem necessary". Gentlemen, in my capacity as Commissioner of this bureau, I believe unnecessary force was used. They were put on to that train at gunpoint.' Argand was quite white now – perhaps because he had been speaking quickly and had become breathless, perhaps because he was about to make a, for him, peculiarly impassioned statement. 'Only once before have I seen men herded on to trains in such a way. In August 1944. The newspaper *Slik Stien* this morning made the same comparison. Normally I abhor *Slik Stien*, but today it was right.

'Excellencies, Chairman, I refer to these cases to establish first that a dangerous, profoundly unhealthy atmosphere, ambience, mood exists in our forces at the moment: they are examples only, my files hold many dozens similar . . .'

'Chairman. I must protest. This really will not do . . .'

Gapp too had lost colour – and the large freckles on his forehead, across his flattish nose, stood out in lurid contrast

Prinz eyed him over his spectacles.

'Be brief please, General.'

'Chairman. Secretary. You cannot surely expect us to sit here and listen to *stuff* about *ambience, mood*. Quite clearly none of us on this committee is going to vote to take action over such nebulous vapourisings . . .'

'General, Commissioner Argand is merely trying to establish background. He will now proceed to facts.'

Argand paused, looked away from his papers at a heavily framed portrait of a nineteenth-century official dressed in a jacket covered with silver leaves and clutching a court sword.

'But this . . . mood *is* important. It is only because a shared atmosphere exists that men can combine, can begin to cover each other's actions. It is the general *tone* that exists in their barracks and stations that forces even the reluctant to condone evil practices. And out of that, inevitably, they will begin to formalise . . .'

'Commissioner. Facts. Now. Please.'

'Very well.' Argand looked down at his papers, blinked, ran a finger down a margin, carefully turned the top sheet over to his right. 'Very well. Now I should like to turn first to the Hotel Bristol and summarise the facts about that. The commune of the Hotel Bristol at Brichtzee was, in the first instance, made up entirely of members of the university branch of the League of Marxist–Leninist Militants. They were raided twice by the Rural Guard. After the first raid several members left, and three new ones joined. They were not students and it has been very difficult for me to establish exactly who they were. For a time I believed, as had members of the original commune, that they were members of Red Spectre or a similar extreme left-wing terrorist group. They brought in and caused to be well hidden a small arsenal of very powerful weapons. They planned to attack The Hok plant, the reactor itself, with heat-guided, hand-launched missiles known as Red-eyes, having got within range using fragmentation grenades, and machine pistols. The attack was to take place during Walter Beck's planned speech announcing the formation of a broad left alliance incorporating anti-nuclear and ecological groups. The plan was aborted by the rain which caused the rally to be moved to St Romain. I shall return to that: but for the moment let us stay with the Hotel Bristol.

'The first thing to note about this terrorist plot is that it was clearly aimed at Beck. The connection between the terrorists and the League would be proved, and between the League and Beck. What the terrorists probably did not know was that Beck had dropped the League from his alliance three days before the rally. Now, one at least of the commune still accepts that the overthrow of Beck could credibly be the aim of Red Spectre. I won't go into all that – the ramifications of left-wing theology would defeat a church father. But when all this came clear to me, the nature of the three terrorists and so on, I found it hard to believe, but my own unwillingness to think the unthinkable still prevented me from forming the only other possible hypothesis.

'I must now go back to the Hotel Bristol and those raids.

'During the third raid, the one carried out by the State Security Police, a map of The Hok plant was found in the possession of a commune member, Wilhelm Koonig. It is a detailed map of the plant's defences, an official one, a photocopy of the one prepared for the detachment of the Mobile Operations Unit which guards the plant. That is also significant and I shall return to it. But for the moment – Koonig. Here are some facts about him. Of the original members of the commune, he was the strongest willed. The son of a railway worker, he was studying politics at the university and was the most active in the League. He had done proper military service and recognised the arms for what they were.

He was trying to get the rest of the commune to expel the three terrorists. That was his position when the third raid took place and he was hit on the head with fatal force by Trooper Kral.

'Now some more facts about the commune. After the first raid, Licentiate Petersen, who had negotiated the lease, requested the commune, and they agreed, to remove anything that could get them into further trouble with the police. There was very little. Some cannabis held in common – that's all. There followed a second raid and nothing illegal whatsoever was found at all. At the third raid the map, which must have been come by illegally, was discovered. There are anomalies here which I must admit did not present themselves to me at the time – then we were only concerned to discover whether or not the raid had been properly authorised and if Kral's assault on Koonig was illegal.'

Argand paused, sipped water. The faces round the table were now expressionless, impassive, and he felt again the little tack-tack-tack of doubt, like a deathwatch beetle gnawing its way into the fabric he was building up: perhaps, after all, it was fantasy, the creature of his paranoia and Prinz's ambition. But no. That would not do. That way madness lies. Best to get on with it.

'Now we move on to the rally. Here are some facts. On their own they don't amount to much, might even seem insignificant. For instance, there is the fact that Excellency Commissioner General Gapp alone objected to moving the rally from the perimeter of The Hok to St Romain . . .'

'This is intolerable.' Gapp struck the table with clenched fist.

Prinz looked up sharply. 'Is it? If so, you have my word that what Commissioner Argand has just said will be struck from the record and he will apologise in full. Meanwhile, we must let him proceed.'

'As I said, here are the facts about the rally at St Romain that I take to be relevant. At 3.41 – incidentally the times I give are exact, taken from photographs that include the town hall clock which was correct to within fifteen seconds as the law concerning public clocks insists – at 3.41 a man, later identified as Mark Robart, one of the three Hotel Bristol terrorists, climbed the flagpole from which the British flag was flying. One of my men, Detective Ensign Focking, seconded from State Security, moved in to arrest him. From the balcony of the town hall, Squadron Commandant Krater, also of State Security, watched what was happening through a pair of first-rate binoculars. He recognised Focking. Focking was not able to get to Robart, who had, by 3.42, cut down the Union Jack and was now beginning his ascent of the central flagpole, the one flying the flag of Brabt.

'At this point Focking was also recognised by Mik Rasp, known as Standen, one of the two homosexuals who had complained to my bureau three weeks earlier. Focking was the officer who investigated that complaint. Rasp was right at the foot of the flagpole as the terrorist descended and Focking moved in to arrest him. At a moment just short of 3.45 Focking was stabbed to death, not by Robart but by a tall, fair-haired man. However, by what seems at first sight to be an outrageous coincidence but was in fact nothing of the sort, Rasp also identified Robart. Not by name but by appearance.

'Rasp and his friend Paul Standen had been intimidated into dropping their complaint by three man who entered their apartment, wrecked it, and beat them. They claimed to be acting in the interest of moral hygiene . . .' Here Argand's voice thickened again with disgust. 'One of them had a tattoo on his right forearm representing the emblem of the Mobile Operations Unit, and extensive goldwork on his upper-left molars. Rasp is convinced that this man and the man whom

Focking was about to arrest at St Romain, that is Mark Robart, were one and the same.

'At 3.45, two hundred State Security Troopers in full riot gear, with cover from CS gas, came down the steps of the town hall in a baton charge. They had been ordered to clear the square – something that anyone at all experienced in crowd control would have realised was impossible under the circumstances without loss of life and severe injury.

'Squadron Commandant Krater admits to giving the order. He says that he did so because he had seen Focking stabbed. But it is now clear that the order was given nearly three minutes earlier. It took that long for his colleague, who logged receipt of the order, to call his Troopers from standby to full alert and then launch them. What lies behind this discrepancy? I shall give my answer to that in a moment.

'I interviewed Krater as part of my general inquiries into the death of Focking on the day after the event, and remained at St Romain for that night, Sunday night. On my way back to Brabt on Monday morning, a clumsy but potentially successful attempt was made on my life . . .' Again he paused, passed a hand over his eyes, hoping to erase the orange cylinder as it bounced up off the concrete. 'This attempt was the work of two men, Jakob Braun and Hans Braun, who it appears are step-brothers, though as yet not much is known about them. Jakob was arrested. Hans got away.

'It was arranged that Jakob should be transferred from Traffic headquarters to Crime for questioning. During the transfer, he apparently tried to escape, although handcuffed, and suffered near-fatal injuries under a bus. This was no more than a temporary reprieve. An unknown man (again the terrifying moment, the masked and gowned figure on the other side of the glass panel, like a reflection of himself, a doppelganger) managed to murder Jakob in the intensive-care unit, in spite of the fact that there was a policeman on the outer door who let him in, in spite of the fact that I myself was sitting at Jakob's bedside.

'Now we must return to Jakob's step . . .'

A knock on the door – the discreet tap of a civil servant.

Prinz looked over his glasses.

'Come.'

'Two documents for Commissioner Stent, sir. I am told he should see them as a matter of urgency.'

'Of course. Commissioner Stent?'

'I can receive them here. No need for me to leave.'

Two large sheets of flimsy printout paper. Stent smoothed them out, glanced over them – lists of names under headings, with short comments. He lifted his heavy head. 'That's all right, Secretary. There really is no need for further interruption. Commissioner Argand can go on.'

Argand took a deep breath. He could not see the papers, but the exchange between Prinz and Stent had been pre-arranged. It seemed things were going well.

'Jakob's step-brother, Hans. There are several facts and a supposition or two I should like you to know about him. He was the bastard son of Jakob's step-mother and took the name Braun when his mother married Jakob's father. But he also uses his original surname on occasion and that has made it difficult for us to trace him. Under the name Braun, he was one of the three terrorists in the Hotel Bristol. He gave evidence of Koonig's fall downstairs at the inquiry. He instructed a joiner sympathetic to the aims of the League to build a hiding-place in the hotel for the weapons. He terror-ised Licentiate Petersen and his friend Lisa Smit into leaving the country. I believe he killed Focking, and his motive was not quite as obvious as it might seem. I believe he engineered the attempt on my life. I believe that he made a second attempt which resulted in the murder of a Belgian doctor who happened to be in a car similar to mine at a time and place where I might have been. The doctor's chauffeur was also killed. It is even possible he killed his step-brother Jakob. At all events, he is an extremely dangerous man, a psychopathic killer. Yet my efforts to trace him have been obstructed in ways I shall describe shortly. There are just two more things about Hans Braun we do know. He has a friend, Mark Robart, with gold bridgework and a MOBOP tattoo on his arm; and there is some evidence, yet to be corroborated, that the weapons hidden in the Hotel Bristol came from MOBOP . . .'

'Ah,' Gapp slapped his hand on the table. 'I think I see where you are leading. Your hypothesis is that the Mobile Operations Unit has been infiltrated by extreme left-wingers. Interesting. Possible even, but most unlikely. Still, if it's the only theory that fits what has been a tendentious presentation of so-called facts, then I can see there is a temptation to embrace it. But I am sure all that you have told us could, seen from a different, wider perspective, be made to fit a quite different pattern, or no pattern at all. These "facts" are so unconnected, so disparate . . .'

Prinz let the voice, harsh and a touch breathless now, fade into silence. Then: 'Commissioner Argand, you have one more cluster of facts?'

Argand nodded, moved a sheet of paper to the pile on his right, leaving only one left. He took breath.

'There is, affiliated to or part of the Friends of Brabt, a secret, closed organisation called the Chevaliers of Christ the Purifier. The first group to go by this name existed in the 1880s and was avowedly anti-semitic. Members of the present group paraded under hoods at the Festival of Moral Regeneration. Focking was a member. He passed on the names of complainants to my bureau to someone in the Friends. As a result, nearly all the complainants were harassed and terrorised into dropping their complaints. It seems that this intimidation was also carried out by Chevaliers. State Security Trooper Kral is a Chevalier. Jakob Braun was one. It seems likely that Hans Braun is also a Chevalier.

'Chairman, Excellencies – that concludes the factual side.'

31

This created a moment of almost involuntary relaxation. Chairs were pushed back, lighters flared, someone coughed, papers were shuffled.

Pranck cleared his throat. 'I must admit, Jan, you've gone too quickly for me. Personally I'd like a transcript of what you've said so far, so I can familiarise myself with it all before hearing your interpretation . . .'

'I must say that is a very sound suggestion.' Wynand jumped in, leant forward. As always, he spoke briskly, gave an impression of intelligence, ability. 'May I propose, Secretary, that we are all given a transcript and meet again in a week's time to hear the next phase. Meanwhile, we could now hear what General Gapp has to say. I can assure you it is a much simpler business.'

Again Prinz's cherubic face quite lost its benign aspect; less of a Buddha, more a minatory if overweight Jove, he tapped the table with his gold lighter.

'All right, Jan,' he said, formalities apparently forgotten. 'Carry on to your conclusion.'

Silence returned, then Gapp swung sideways in his chair as if he were about to get up, but fell back on one elbow, his head raised, looking with studied exasperation at the large, velvet-draped window beyond Prinz's head.

'I think I can now be brief.' Argand pushed his papers to one side, spoke carefully but without notes.

'For reasons I would not care to have to explain' – he was

thinking of that side of man that is irredeemably evil, of the never-ending struggle between good and bad, light and dark, that he took to be the mainspring of history – 'that mood, ambience, atmosphere I spoke of to begin with has grown like an evil fog in certain sections of our society. Out of it, bit by bit, cells of like-minded people have come together – in some cases, poisoning existing organisations in themselves tremendously promising, with fine and noble aims like the Friends of Brabt and the Festival of Moral Regeneration; in others, forming new groups, albeit under old names like the Chevaliers of Christ the Purifier.

'This last group has extensive membership in our police forces and also in the Mobile Operations Unit. Using state institutions, facilities provided by the state, and using the state as a cover, it has embarked on a wicked campaign of harassment and intimidation of minority groups: Jews, guest workers, homosexuals, left-wingers, eccentrics and so on. I recall that General Gapp, at an earlier meeting of this committee, called for a reappraisal of our role as policemen. He said' – here Argand closed his eyes, pinched the bridge of his nose and then repeated by heart – ' "We must grasp a quite new awareness of ourselves as the active and instituted guardians of social hygiene." I fear that is precisely what the Chevaliers believe themselves to be about. At all events, we must take immediate steps to identify every member of our forces who belongs to this sect and suspend them immediately – until a full inquiry has been carried out by an independent body. Perhaps we should ask our Belgian and Dutch colleagues to assist us.

'Serious indeed though the activities of the Chevaliers in general have been, far more serious is what I take to be a conspiracy or plot to destroy Walter Beck and the new leftward movement of the Reformed Socialist Party. Interpreting the facts I have given you, this is what I believe has been happening.

210

'Three Chevaliers, or sympathisers, Hans Braun and the Robart brothers, who have served in the Mobile Operations Unit and still have close connections with it, infiltrated the Hotel Bristol commune, giving its members to understand that they were left-wing terrorists. Their plan was to mount, to stage an attack on The Hok reactor at the very moment when Beck was due to announce the alliance of the Reformed Socialists with, amongst others, groups like the League of Marxist–Leninist Militants.

'In the run-up to the rally, they found Wilhelm Koonig an embarrassment, a potential danger. Braun attempted to intimidate him by pushing him down the stairs and no doubt in other ways too. He suffered more serious injury at the hands of Chevalier State Security Trooper Kral during the third raid, and the MOBOP defence plan of The Hok which had been planted on him was "discovered". This, of course, would serve to complete the case against the League as the originators of the attack on the reactor. I should have realised something like this was afoot much earlier. From the start there was no *sound* reason for the third raid after the second had been unproductive.

'The rain at The Hok aborted everything. The rally moved to St Romain. An alternative plan to disrupt Beck and bring his alliance into immediate discredit was hastily improvised: the plan to implicate the League in the destruction of the flags and the riot which would appear to follow. Nothing like as good as the first plan but something completely new had to be put together in a matter of hours.

'Exactly *why* what happened took place is still a matter of conjecture. But one thing is certain. Krater ordered the baton charge both before Focking died and, more oddly, before the riot which the conspirators hoped would build up after the Brabanter flag had been torn down was properly under way.

211

'Focking was a Chevalier. Such organisations are secretive. It is likely that he knew only the members of his cell. However, he would be known to senior members. Krater says that he recognised Focking as a police officer because he had met him briefly in the town hall before the rally. I think it more likely that he knew Focking as a State Trooper and Chevalier before he joined my bureau.

'Focking was not a knowing part of the conspiracy against Beck. He hated left-wingers, was, in a rather simple way, a patriot. He moved in to arrest Mark Robart, the man who was pulling down the flags. Krater observed what was about to happen and launched the baton charge prematurely to give Robart a chance of escape. Why? Because, if Focking had succeeded in arresting Robart, it could well have been revealed that Robart was a past or present member of the Chevaliers and MOBOP, and the whole plot to discredit the left would blow up in their faces. Meanwhile, in the interval between Krater's order and the actual charge, Braun moves in to protect his friend for much the same reasons and, since Focking is a determined and strong man, stabs him to death.'

Argand paused, looked round, eyes suddenly strained. Some inner censor had caught and reprimanded his uncharacteristically dramatic use of the present tense and caused him visibly to take a grip on himself. He shook his head, sipped water and continued but more slowly, in a more restrained way.

'The day after these events I questioned Krater – and, while at the time I had no idea that this was the case, sufficiently alarmed him and his colleagues to prompt them to obstruct my inquiries in a variety of ways. The two attempts on my life are clear enough. But so too is the blocking of my attempt to have the Hotel Bristol forensically examined after one of my men had questioned a witness who had seen the

212

weapons there. Why was this done? One remembers that fingerprints are now computer-filed and every member past and present of the security forces including MOBOP has his prints on those files. The quartermaster of MOBOP refused to tell me if weapons were missing from his armouries. The warrant-issuing magistrate was intimidated and letter-bombed.

'I am nearly through. I do not think the attempted murder of Jakob Braun, nor his actual murder, could have been accomplished without the connivance of one or more police officers. Serenity Vustouk received threatening letters after he had privately indicated to the State Prosecutor's office that Chevalier Kral should be charged with the culpable homicide of Koonig – an indication, I think, that there is at least one Chevalier in State Prosecution.

'Chairman, Gentlemen. I invite you to endorse this inter-pretation of the facts. A shadowy network of right-wing activists, based on the Chevaliers of Christ the Purifier, has subverted a significant number of officers, particularly in the Mobile Operations Unit, the State Security Police and the Rural Guard; that these men have committed what General Gapp, at an earlier meeting, called the greatest blasphemy of all – they have denied the state's monopoly of violence. I propose that all operations by MOBOP and State Security be suspended and all officers and men confined to barracks or headquarters until an investigative inquiry has been completed; that similar steps should be taken against the Rural Guard, excepting only that such policing as is necessary for the safety of the civil population outside the City boundaries should be maintained.'

At last Argand leant back, head in the air, eyes briefly closed. Then he glanced round the white, set faces opposite him – Gapp indeed seemed almost to have gone grey, shadows had appeared round his eyes, the skin on his face had tightened, giving it a skull-like appearance.

Prinz was brisk: 'Excellency Stent, Commissioner for Prevention and Detection of Crime will second the proposal.'

As Stent began, his voice loud and deep, Argand at last really did relax, his chin dropped towards his chest, the fists on the table slowly opened.

'Chairman, Excellencies. During the course of this meeting I have received information which is relevant to the matters we are discussing.' With large hands he smoothed out the thin printout paper in front of him. 'Acting on a warrant issued on the basis of evidence of extortion with menaces and forgery presented by one Sarah Frankel against the Friends of Brabt, a detachment of my men today raided the headquarters of that organisation. Amongst many other documents of significance to what we have just heard, a list of the entire membership of the Chevaliers of Christ the Purifier and a sister group called the Handmaids of the Lord has been recovered. It seems there are forty-three Chevaliers in State Security, including Squadron Commandant Krater, and twenty-eight in the Rural Guard. There are also fifteen in Traffic, eight in Public Order, eight – I am sorry to say – in Crime, and two in the Bureau of Advice and Investigation. A further thirty-three occupy administrative and clerical posts in government departments, and a further one hundred and ninety-six are in occupations not directly related to the state.

'The situation in the Mobile Operations Unit is more serious. Hans Braun, under his mother's name, is a serving sergeant; the name Robart is also assumed, but we believe we have pinpointed two corporals who are Chevaliers and fit the descriptions we have of the brothers who went under that name at the Hotel Bristol. In all, twenty-three soldiers and four officers serving with MOBOP are implicated and there may be more. The connivance of very many people would have been necessary for these three men to have been absent, for the weapons to be released, and so on. Already many of the people on these lists have been arrested or, where rank seemed to make less extreme measures appropriate, have been asked to remain in their homes. However, the men we have heard described as Braun and Robart have so far evaded capture.

'I second Excellency Commissioner Argand's proposal and most earnestly endorse particularly the suggestion that all Mobile Operations Unit operations should be suspended, and personnel, all personnel, confined to barracks pending the completion of a fuller inquiry.'

'Thank you, Excellency Stent. Does anyone wish to speak against the proposal.'

Gapp's mottled white hand unfolded itself from the table, stood up, it seemed, without its owner's volition. Prinz gave it a slow nod. Gapp's voice was quiet now, the words spaced.

'Chairman, we have been presented with a crazy structure of fairytale-like substance, based on an arbitrary choice of unconnected and distorted facts. The Chevaliers of Christ the Purifier and the Handmaids of the Lord are perfectly legitimate societies of respectable people with nothing but the very best interests of our City and Province at heart. The honour of our dedicated police forces has been grossly, horribly impugned. Men of distinguished parentage, from families like the Kraters who have centuries of selfless public service behind them, have been made the victims of what I can only suppose is a communist . . .'

'Please speak to the motion.'

Gapp shook his head as if responding to a foul taste in his mouth. 'It would be the grossest breach of public safety to withdraw the Mobile Operations Unit from service. Nuclear installations at The Hok, the NATO air base, and, if I may raise the proposal I was to put to this meeting, the imminence of a large rally which will put on to the streets of the City precisely those elements of the populace our state has most reason to fear . . .'

With clearly calculated rudeness, Prinz prised dross from the bowl of his pipe. The gold blade of his knife scraped squeakily, and he looked up as Gapp paused.

'I need hardly remind you that this committee's function is purely advisory. Cognisant as I was of most of what Argand has told us, I yesterday evening called an extraordinary meeting of the Council of State.' The Secretary began to thumb tobacco. 'As you know, in the absence of the Grand Duke, and with the Moot not sitting, the Council has authority to take any temporary measures it chooses to ensure that the continuing government of the state should be effective. The full Council was present. That is: Count Frederick as Regent, the Prime Minister, the Deputy Prime Minister, the Secretary of Defence, and myself. We took several measures and one in particular which should reassure General Gapp. The Grand Duke's Own First Armoured Division, deployed normally on the Rhine near Köln, is at this moment falling back on Brabt via motorways which the Federal German and Dutch governments have kindly made clear for us. By' – Prinz looked at his watch – 'yes, by now, forward companies will have taken over all duties normally carried out by the Mobile Operations Unit.'

Gapp hissed. 'So. After all, this has been a charade.'

Prinz slowly lit his pipe, beamed at last through the smoke. 'Not entirely, General. This meeting has served a purpose. And I now declare it closed.'

As most of the others began to leave, Argand leaned towards

Stent and drew the printout in across the deeply polished mahogany.

Silently Stent indicated the two names from the Bureau of Advice and Investigation implicated with the Chevaliers. One, of course, was expected. But, as he read the second, Argand for a moment felt a stab of anguish, quite surprisingly sharp, but it was only for a moment. The tiny emotional explosion died and left only the bitter fumes of a resigned recognition that this also was something he should have guessed.

Stent murmured, 'Leave that one in place, eh?'

Argand's large arched eyebrows rose yet higher.

Stent went on, 'I think so. Hans Braun has already been in contact. He might again. So. A good lead. After all he must be caught.'

Argand rubbed his palms in his eyes then nodded briskly. 'Yes, yes of course. There'll be a full surveillance. And you'll let me know how I can help.'

At the end of the table Prinz zipped up his document case, snapped the gold lock, came round the table and joined them.

'Is this wise, Piet? Is not this, er, in some measure using Jan as a tethered goat?'

'Well, yes. But that remains the case anyway, until Braun and the Robarts are pulled in. We'll take very good care of him, I assure you.'

'I'm sure you will.' Prinz took Argand's elbow and they moved towards the large double oak doors. 'But will Jan take proper care of himself?' The subtlest shift of his face muscles somehow conveyed a touch of sincerity that might not have been there before. 'Take care, Commissioner. Take care.'

Then he chuckled. 'After all, I doubt if they'll allow it to count in your favour that you once sent a quite large cheque yourself to the Friends of Brabt, eh? Well?'

The pressure on Argand's elbow increased slightly then was gone. Huge head sunk between huge shoulders, pipe-smoke billowing round him, the Secretary stumped off down the deeply carpeted corridor. Beneath the glitter of chandeliers, he looked almost as Churchillian as he imagined himself to be.

32

'You are acquainted with Dr Brunot, I believe. Our Reader in Spanish Literature.'

'Yes. I met her in the Virtue Islands. When I was advising on internal security for the American base there.' Argand frowned – the memory of the sturdy but attractive academic who had got under his skin in several ways was not a comfortable one.

'Yes. She speaks well of you. Apparently you forestalled a right-wing coup there too.'

Argand stopped. A second later, Catedratika Arendt did too. They stood facing each other across a metre or two of fallen chestnut leaves. The vast black trunk of one of them was almost within Arendt's reach and a huge spear-shaped leaf of bright gold swung gently past her shoulder. Around and below them the University Park dropped away through more chestnuts, oaks and beeches to the new campus. Only the chestnuts and a copse of silver birches had so far turned – the oaks and beeches were as green as they had been six weeks before.

'There was no question of a coup here.' Argand spoke firmly.

'No? Most of the gossip has it that that man Gapp wanted MOBOP and the Troopers into the City for just that purpose.'

'That's not true. He requested their presence. In case of trouble on the march or at the rally. The request was turned down.'

Arendt shrugged, swung away. She was dressed in what looked like a man's tweed jacket over a roll-neck sweater and flannel trousers.

'It's true,' Argand insisted. 'He would hardly be where he is now if he had been planning treason.'

'Brabanter ambassador to NATO? Well. He has powerful friends. Very powerful. And Brussels is too near for my peace of mind.'

They walked on in silence, not wishing to disagree so often, though it was difficult not to. The truth was that they liked each other, wanted the acquaintance to grow into friendship, but it was difficult for either to speak without provoking at least a minor confrontation.

'You know,' Arendt said at last, 'this used to be the Grand Dukes' deer forest.'

'Of course.' Argand thought of the pageantry of a medieval or Renaissance court out hunting: the horns, the baying hounds, the bright caparisons, neighing steeds, ladies in steeple hats with hooded hawks on their wrists. It seemed a shame that it was now a public park used for the most part by students. There was some litter, though not much, and he had not been able to avoid noticing a used contraceptive.

'This spot always gives me the shudders.' Arendt gestured over a declivity, almost treeless, about half a kilometre in length, two hundred metres across. Because it was sheltered from the cool breeze and the sun shone fitfully, there were fifty or so students in it, mostly in couples, some on their own and reading, and at one end five or six played volleyball over an imagined net.

'Why?'

'This is where the actual hunting took place. If you can call it that. The poor beasts were herded into pens at that end, the dukes, counts, barons, foreign ambassadors and so on stood just below where we are now, and at twenty-minute intervals the deer were sent through, five or six at a time. They used crossbows in the early days, guns from 1560 onwards. I have a student who has calculated that half a million beasts died down there. It's a better scene now.'

They stepped out down the gentle slope. It had been Arendt's idea, this walk. She had not forgotten how the Commissioner had shared her appreciation of the early September sunset, how she had mentioned the coming glory of the autumnal chestnuts. Argand had accepted, glad to get out. For five weeks he had moved only in bullet- and rocket-proof cars, and always shadowed by carefully screened gunmen, for the informer in his bureau remained there and Braun and the Robarts were still at large. Then, just three days before Arendt's call, the Spanish Secret Police in Madrid had raided a cell of the *Guerrilleros de Cristo Rey*, probably in a routine way to keep the democratised Cortes happy, and had actually stumbled on almost all the MOBOP missing arms – and the Robart brothers who had been trying to sell them. From that day, against Prinz's advice, Argand's life had returned to something like normal, though he was still shadowed by a discreet bodyguard.

Prompted by Arendt's version of courtly hunting, a melancholy settled in Argand's mind; it deepened as they passed a litter bin that had been fly-posted 'A Free Brabt needs Free Chevaliers'. It was marked with the black-barred tilted cross that was so near to being a swastika.

'It's a terrible thing,' he reflected aloud, 'the black part of us. It's like a disease. You can root it out, cut it back, but you can't destroy it. It'll always come back one way or another. I suppose there will always be very evil men too, who will recognise it in all of us, exploit it, organise it . . .'

Arendt had stopped. They were almost on the floor of the declivity now. He realised that something he had done or said had made her very angry.

'The fact,' she said, 'that decent people like you can believe such mystical rubbish does as much as anything to keep the thing going.'

'Oh.'

'Yes.'

'Well?'

'Do you want to know the truth of it?'

He shrugged. 'Of course.'

She pulled a plastic pack-mac from her pocket, unfolded it, spread it on the grass – still dry and brownish from the summer which, apart from the storm at the end of August, had been a good one – and sat on it. There was not room for Argand too – at least not without sitting closer to her than he felt he could. He unfolded the copy of *The Brabanter* he was carrying and sat on that, almost facing her. He hoped she would not take too long: he feared sciatica more than anything . . .

'Fascism,' she began, 'is not the product of black mystical forces, and to explain it thus is to play right into their hands. It is appalling how many apparently sensible people believe that sort of drivel. And many liberal intellectuals are as bad: they talk about man's anti-social disposition, his natural aggression, as if these were facts; or, worse still, just throw up their hands in despair and write fascism off as a sport, an aberration, a disease.'

She seemed to have stopped, was collecting her thoughts perhaps. One hundred, one hundred and fifty metres away, on the crest behind them, a man sat down, and with his arms across his knees looked out over their heads. Argand wondered if it was Tremp who that day was on duty as his minder.

'How else explain?' he said. 'The Chevaliers had a branch for women. The Handmaids of the Lord. There's one in my office. She's devout. In many ways kind. Thrifty. Hard-

222

working, not stupid. Why should she be . . . one of those?'

'A fascist?'

He nodded though he disliked using such an extreme term for Petra Madjen. Her continued presence in the office was a source of dull pain to Argand. She was so good . . . Yet she had passed on the information about his whereabouts which had led to the bombing of the Belgian doctor's Peugeot, and had presumably agreed to betray the murdered Focking so her own presence as a spy in the bureau might remain undetected. And she stayed on, ignorant of the surveillance she was under, and Stent waited for Braun to contact her.

Inevitably Julia Arendt had her explanation and, as Argand continued privately to mourn the corruption of people like Madjen, the lecture continued.

'Fascism is a product of post-industrial, late capitalist society. This is how it happens. Advanced countries need a vast army of clerks, management, technicians, skilled artisans, and, most important of all, functionaries in their millions to service the great bureaucracies – whether they be industrial or financial corporations, local or state or international governments like the EEC. The system depends on this army, which often accounts for as many as a third of the population, and so they are tied into it by every means possible. They are well rewarded, but their rewards depend on acceptance of competitiveness and psychic violence as natural. Through education and the media, they are ideologically conditioned to accept as virtuous such traits as ambition, acquisitiveness, compulsive working, the rights of the individual over and against the group. They are taught to accept the vicarious violence of neo-colonial wars, that the small nuclear family is the natural unit to live in, and so on. In most states all this is heavily shored up by religion, by a fierce sort of nationalism, and by social sciences based on a vulgar social Darwinism, and by behaviourism – the

223

psychology of rewards and punishments.

'Now capitalism as a mode of production is constantly threatened by its own inner contradictions which will lead eventually and inevitably either to worldwide socialism under the dictatorship of the proletariat, through revolution, or to nuclear holocaust.'

Argand flinched. It was when the Catedratika, who was now also Dean, used this sort of terminology that he felt most uncomfortable with her. He suspected that she knew this, and did it on purpose. At all events she ignored his obvious distaste and pushed on.

'As the crisis deepens, as successive crises become worse, this class I am describing is threatened in ways it cannot understand, and can do little about. Its standard of living falls, unemployment begins to bite. Its members react, in one of two ways. A minority drop out, temporarily anyway they become ecologists, nuclear protesters, eat whole food. They may even see that their interests have more in common with the proletariat, especially that of the Third World, than with their own bourgeoisie, and they become left-wingers of one sort or another: Trots, Maoists; and those whose lives have been most completely alienated and dehumanised by their upbringing become left-wing terrorists. Professional conspirators is what Marx calls them.'

Glancing up over her shoulder, Argand realised that the man on the crest had moved slightly – it was after all not Tremp. This man was taller, possibly fair, apparently a musician of some sort – the Conservatoire was not far away – for he had, Argand could now see, what looked like a case for a musical instrument.

'The majority, however, will push themselves, or allow themselves to be pushed, even more deeply into the dreadful ideological snakepit they have been born and brought up in. They will reassert more strongly than ever the goodness of

224

the nuclear family and will savagely react to attacks on it through sexual permissiveness or women's liberation. They will accept the overt teaching of their bourgeois leaders and will support vicious suppression of the workers, calling for limitations of trade unions' rights and so on. As the crisis deepens, they will turn on racial minorities and blame them for what is happening: Jews, coloured immigrants from ex-colonies, guest workers brought in during the boom years.

'And there comes a point when the bourgeois themselves are forced to accept the danger they are in. In the earlier phase, with increasing unemployment, workers will accept a lower standard of living rather than face the sack. Strikes become rarer and are easily broken. But when unemployment reaches twenty per cent or even less the social fabric begins to come apart. There are spontaneous riots. Union membership rises again. The social democrat parties that claim to represent the workers are forced to move left or split. The calls for a radical change, for revolution, come not from isolated groups of intellectuals and professional discontents, but more and more from the working people as a whole.

'At this point fascism is born, or, more correctly, is created. Covertly the bourgeois begin to encourage the class of which I have been speaking to form nationalist, mass-supported parties whose specific aim will be to crush the growing radicalisation of the working class . . .'

It was not a musical instrument. It was a Beretta sub-machine-gun. Used as a machine-gun, it would not be accurate at the range, but at forty rounds of 9-mm parabellum in twenty seconds it would not need to be.

'. . . Naturally it is again the case that those whose minds have been most deeply warped by the alienation and violence of their backgrounds . . .'

Alternatively, with its metal stock unfolded, and using

single-shot firing at two shots every three seconds, it could be as accurate as a rifle.

'. . . will emerge as leaders. What's the matter?'

'I think that man up there is about to kill me.'

Arendt gave a short nervous laugh.

'Oh dear. And I thought I was boring you. What do we do now?'

'I think you should lie as flat as you can on your stomach with your arms covering your head.'

'I will do no such thing.'

Argand stood, walked briskly away from her, trying to put as much distance between them as he could. But she followed, caught his arm, indeed to his horror he realised she was trying to place herself between him and the gunman.

As he pushed her roughly away, three shots rang out. The man twisted on one foot as if caught in a huge gust of wind, then struck by a heavy but invisible door. The gun spun from him. He fell to one knee, tried to straighten, then collapsed to the grass like a marionette whose strings have been cut.

Argand ran up the slope, but Tremp was there first, appearing over the crest, grasping his Browning automatic in both hands.

'Keep away, Chief, please keep away,' he shouted, then crouched to fire again from close range into Braun's head.

For a moment the two men stood, white-faced, over the dead body. One lean arm was stretched out so that the cuff was pulled back to reveal a tattooed scroll: '. . . No Man.' Six inches from the hand lay an olive-green egg-shaped grenade, with lettering in bright yellow round the top half. The firing ring and lever seemed still to be at safety.

Panting slightly, Julia Arendt came up behind them.

Argand turned, shouted, 'For God's sake keep away.'

He meant because of the grenade; she thought because of

the horror that Braun had now become. Most of his head had been blown apart.

She took off her jacket and slung it over the mess.

'There is no mystery about death,' she said, 'but there are young people around. They should not see such things.' Then she straightened, pushed a wisp of iron-grey hair out of her eyes, which were bright and, Argand realised, angry. 'And no mystery about fascism either.'

33

November. Across a landscape whose desolation could not have been aggravated even by nuclear attack, Commissioner Argand allowed himself to be driven. Bare flat fields. No trees, no hedges. The brutal architecture of a modern trunk road. A flat sky of purple cloud that promised but withheld the benison that snow would bring to such a place. Then a change. Four kilometres away across the dull expanse black trees arose round what had once been a château, and Argand's heart sank as always it did at this point, for it was the third Sunday and the stately home ahead was Hearts Haven.

He flicked over the folded copy of *The Brabanter* that lay across his knee, and with feelings of boredom overlaying a sharper depression rehearsed again the already far too familiar headlines and reports.

Moot hung again. No overall majority. Parties of the right and the right wing of the PBDC routed. But nine PBDC members always known to be on the left of the party agree to give the Reformed Socialists conditional support. Grand Duke Wilhelm invites Beck to form a government. Secretary Prinz urged to remain at the Ministry of Internal Affairs.

Baron de Merle welcomes the new government – a EUREAC spokesperson has said that the moderation and experience of the PBDC members would be a check on the extremist elements amongst the socialists, meanwhile a measure of controlled reflation would do wonders for the stagnant economy.

Rumours of a romance between Walter Beck and Dean Julia Arendt have been confirmed and an engagement will shortly be announced. Dean Arendt campaigned vigorously for . . .

The big black official car swept through the gates and Commissioner Argand pushed the paper into his briefcase.

He found his wife in the orangery at the back of the house. Maria Argand was sitting, or had been sat, in a large wicker-work chair which yet was too small for her; she was surrounded by ferns and citrus plants in ceramic pots, looked like some rain-forest monster kept for ever by the leaf canopy from the sunlight. Argand found a smaller chair nearby and sat opposite her. Sweat glistened on her blown-up cheeks and the smell of it, sharpened perhaps by urine, hung round her like the atmospheric envelope of a vast planet.

For two seconds her eyes, baleful as ever, held his and his flinched away. After that, she barely acknowledged his presence. Weighed down with the futility of what he was doing, Argand laboriously recapitulated the recent political news. He span it out, conscious there would be little else to talk about when he was done. Her fingers, like *boudins blancs*, picked away at loose threads in her lap, and behind the monotonous drone of his own voice Argand recalled that for a time she had embroidered samplers. Apparently that sort of occupational therapy was no longer part of her regimen, or she was no longer able to do it.

'Well,' he said at last, having exhausted his recollection of *The Brabanter*'s analysis of the political situation, 'one effect of all this is that yet again I am to be given a new job.' He paused. No response. 'From January I am to be seconded to Eurocompol.' Again the pause. 'It's the organisation that liaises the separate police forces of the EEC and particularly advises them on interpretation and enforcement of EEC regulations and decrees. I shall have to commute to Brussels every day. Or get a flat there.' He sighed. 'Well, I expect it to be dull. But I'm glad really. I did not one bit like the Bureau of Advice and Investigation. Not one bit. Though in the end I think we did a good job. The thinking now is that there's no more need for it, so we must have done. Anyway, it's to be run down.'

He looked out over the deserted lawns, to the sunhouses and gazebos where he had sat with her . . . what, six months ago? He had tried then to get her to understand what it was the bureau was to do. And now it was all over and she was still here, as if nothing had happened, nothing at all, as if reality was something locked in her skull and everything outside a dream. Then she stirred. Her voice was thick. She spat on plosives.

'You had a secret. . . a secretary. A woman. P-P-Petra something. You told me about her.

'Yes?'

'I suppose . . . she will go to Brussels with you?'

'No.'

'Oh?'

He looked up at her now. She had turned her huge head away a little, and there was a sort of defensive slyness in both her posture and tone which was both repulsive and pitiable.

'Oh? But. But you thought highly of her. You said so. I th-thought . . .'

'She has left the public service.' Argand spoke haughtily now, was brusque, dismissive. 'She has taken early retirement. I believe she works for Archbishop Oldbrod and the Authentic Catholic Church of Brabt.'

Silence. Then his wife sniggered. Argand braced himself, recognising the signal for one of the outrageous obscenities she occasionally attacked him with.

'Couldn't get it up for her then, is that it? And she's gone

230